EDDIE RED
UNDERCOVER

EDDIE RED
UNDERCOVER
MYSTERY ON MUSEUM MILE

MARCIA WELLS

ILLUSTRATED BY MARCOS CALO

HOUGHTON MIFFLIN HARCOURT
BOSTON   NEW YORK

www.hmhco.com

The text of this book is set in Adobe Garamond Pro.
The illustrations were digitally created using Corel Painter software.

Library of Congress Cataloging-in-Publication Data
Wells, Marcia.
Eddie Red Undercover: Mystery on Museum Mile / by Marcia Wells ; illustrated
by Marcos Calo.
p. cm.
Summary: "Sixth-grader Edmund Xavier Lonnrot, code name
'Eddie Red,' has a photographic memory and talent for drawing anything he sees.
When the NYPD is stumped by a mastermind art thief, Eddie becomes their
secret weapon to solve the case." — Provided by publisher.
ISBN 978-0-544-23833-6
[1. Drawing — Fiction. 2. Memory — Fiction. 3. Art thefts — Fiction.
4. New York (N.Y.) — Fiction. 5. Mystery and detective stories.]
I. Calo, Marcos, illustrator. II. Title.
PZ7.W4663Ed 2014
[Fic] — dc23
2013024153

Manufactured in U.S.A.
DOC 10 9 8 7 6 5 4 3 2 1
4500459917

To Ben,
for everything.

And to Beth and Drew,
for everything else.

DEAD MEAT

———

"State your name."

"Eddie Red."

The officer looks up at me and frowns. "State your real name. For the police report." He jabs a meaty finger at the paperwork in front of him.

"Edmund Lonnrot," I reply, making sure to keep my voice steady despite my wobbly insides. Worst Night Ever.

He sighs. "I suppose you have a middle name?"

Now, I know for a fact there are at least a dozen

secret files in this office with my name on them (middle name included), so either this guy doesn't have security clearance or he's strict about official procedure. Judging from the hard glint in his eyes, he's not going to appreciate any comments I might have on the matter.

"Oh," I say lamely. "Xavier."

He rubs his temples, clearly counting to ten in his head the way he's supposed to when it comes to dealing with children.

"All right, Mr. 'O Xavier,' here's how this works: I'm going to tell you what *we* know, and then you're going to tell me what *you* know. I expect your full cooperation."

I nod.

"We have a detective in the hospital. We've got a smashed van, suspects in custody, and a street in chaos. And we've got you, a material witness covered in blood. Does that sound about right?"

I nod again. Misery.

He sits back in his chair, tapping a pen on the desk. I half expect him to shine one of those bright lights in my eyes like they do in the movies. Instead he just starts chewing on the pen cap, swishing it around in his mouth, reminding me of a cow chomping on its cud.

"I want to know what happened," he snaps, his count-to-ten demeanor cracking.

I gaze at the desk, numb. Where's the trauma counselor? The psychiatric attention? I've been through a lot tonight.

When I don't respond, he starts a lecture a mile long about what he can do to me if I don't answer his questions: hold me there indefinitely, take me to court—to jail even. Maybe the jail for grownups, and wouldn't that be a horrible thing to have happen?

This guy has nothing on my mother. She and my dad are going to skin me alive. And as far as Detective Bovano is concerned, I am dead meat. He's going to grind me into burger, serve up Edmund patties to his buddies.

"Why didn't you tell anyone about the stakeout?" the officer shouts, full on angry now. Policemen usually don't yell at kids like this, but I've broken about two million laws tonight, so I guess I have it coming. The kicker is, I did tell someone. Detective Bovano. A fat lot of good that did him.

Thinking of the detective snaps me out of my stupor. I put on my extra-polite voice, the one I reserve for church, weddings, and funerals; there may be a dead body by the end of this conversation. "I would like to speak with Bovano. He's my supervisor."

"Yeah, great. Sure. Except he's in the hospital. Gunshot wound. You know, the bullet that could have killed you?"

"Is he going to be okay?" My voice cracks. They told me it wasn't serious, but maybe they lied. If anything's happened, then it's all my fault.

Officer Molino (finally I have read the nameplate on his desk) scratches the short black hair on his head. Come to think of it, he's sort of a younger version of Detective Bovano: bulky, Italian, and perpetually irritated at the world. Although, unlike Bovano, this guy seems to have a soft spot for kids with crackly voices.

"He's fine. The bullet just grazed his chest. You can see him this weekend if you want." He offers me a small smile.

I relax my shoulders and start to breathe a little easier. *Bovano isn't dead, Edmund. You stopped the bleeding. You helped him.*

"I still need answers," Molino pushes, more gently this time.

"Have you called my parents?"

He nods. "They know you're safe, but you can't speak with them until we're done here. You signed away your rights when you joined the force—you know that." He leans forward, eyeballing me. "Just answer the questions, Edmund."

I put my head in my hands. I'm not trying to be difficult, but I'm exhausted. And extremely nervous about the impending parental wrath, not to mention feeling guilty about Detective Bovano. "I'm tired," I say. "It's nine at night, my parents are going to kill me, and I just want to go home. Can't we talk about this tomorrow morning?"

The officer shakes his head. "It's gotta be tonight. While it's fresh."

I sigh, smelling defeat. "What do you want to know?"

"Everything."

"Where should I start?"

"How about at the beginning, hmm?" he says, holding his pen ready above the desk.

"All right, but I'd like to have some water, please. And an orange soda. I need some sugar if I'm going to get through this."

He stares at me, mouth open in disbelief, and then

he caves. Muttering something under his breath, he turns and signals to someone across the room.

I smile. Orange soda, a forbidden beverage at my house, is on its way.

I shouldn't be here. I should be at home watching a movie, hanging out with my best friend and doing normal things that eleven-year-olds do, like wrestling until a lamp breaks or making things explode in the microwave.

But instead, I'm Eddie Red. And I am in a lot of trouble.

Chapter 1

FROZEN

If you're a kid, there are three things you need in order to solve a police investigation:

1. A unique crime-fighting talent
2. A best friend who's a genius
3. A boatload of dumb luck

The dumb luck began with an ice cream cone on the Upper East Side during a January thaw.

The term *January thaw* is a lie, at least in New York City. The forecasters tell you it will be fifty degrees out and everybody gets all excited, and gullible kids like me wear shorts to school. But what they don't tell you is that the wind chill will be negative ten and the sun will only be out for three hours, so in the end it all balances out to a nice thirty degrees on the street. I've had goose bumps the size of icebergs all day. At least my mom made me wear my winter jacket.

"I'll have pistachio, please," I say to the lady behind the counter. The ice cream shop is warm and cheerful, with sunny paintings on the wall of kids playing Frisbee in the park and swimming at the beach.

The fact that it's January also means that the ice cream has been sitting there undisturbed since October, so in ice cream years that's about eighty. The woman goes elbow-deep into the tub of pistachio and forces the dregs of the barrel into a cone. Dregs that are covered in freezer burn. My suspicions are confirmed: this ice cream is going to be über-stale.

"I'll have the same," a deep voice echoes behind me. My dad. He smiles down at me, one of his enormous hands coming to rest on my shoulder, the other adjusting the thick glasses that lie across the bridge of his nose.

"I love pistachio," he says, speaking to the woman, who is clearly Not Interested.

"It tastes good," he continues, "but I'm always more keen on what color it's going to be. It isn't naturally green, but because the pistachio nut itself is green, people expect the ice cream to be green like they do with mint. Which isn't naturally green either.

"So the companies add green food dye to it. You never know quite what you're going to get. Ooh!" he exclaims as she hands him the cone. "Today's is positively neon! I think we could call it plutonium!"

The woman's brow crinkles and she gets that startled expression on her face like most people do when they meet my dad. He looks like a three-hundred-pound linebacker who can wrestle a bull with his bare hands, and yet he's in a sweater vest and bow tie (not on my recommendation, believe me).

When he opens his mouth to speak, I don't know if people are expecting a caveman because of his size or what, but usually within thirty seconds it becomes clear that Dad truly knows everything about everything, from the weather patterns in the Amazon to quantum physics to food dye in pistachio ice cream. It's part of his job.

Cones in hand, we leave the shop and head down a quieter street toward an empty park bench. I sit and watch the traffic trickle by, trying to ignore the gloom brewing in my stomach. Ice cream out with Dad usually means one thing: serious conversations involving bad news. Like the time when he told me that my hamster Leviticus had been trapped and eaten by Sadie, our evil cat. That day involved some cookies 'n' cream and a whole lot of tissues.

"Edmund," my father says quietly, hailing the arrival of the Moment of Reckoning. My stomach does a somersault. All breathing stops.

I should be on a bus headed over to the Upper West Side, where we live. I wish I were on that bus. I'd be a lot warmer. And calmer.

"Edmund, they've cut my hours back at the library again. I'm going to search for a different job, but in this economy . . ." He lets the sentence hang there. I know where this is going. I've heard the rumblings at home. I don't want to hear what he's going to say next, so I take a big lick of my ice cream in a desperate attempt to distract my brain. Yuck. Gurgly things start happening to my already churning digestive tract.

"I'm sorry," he says, "but we can't send you back to Senate next year. We just can't afford it. You'll have to switch schools. But don't worry," he adds, patting my hand. "You'll make new friends. And you can visit Jonah on the weekends."

No more Senate Academy? The words wash over me, fizzing on my skin like a bad rash. No more awesome classes like architecture and photography and fencing? No more bus rides or bagel breakfast sandwiches with Jonah? Or blowing things up in chem lab with Jonah or eating at Al's Pizza after school with Jonah?

"What about a loan?" I ask. "I'll do anything. I'll get an afterschool job." Who would hire an eleven-year-old? Maybe the Mafia . . . they have kids run errands for them all the time in the movies. "I'll pay you back, plus interest. We have to talk to Mom. She'll know how to fix it."

Icy wind pricks at my eyes, making them water. Just then a woman walks by in a pink scarf, her green eyes widening with sympathy. Great, she thinks I'm crying. I wipe the frozen tears away quickly. All I need is for someone from my class to witness this and I'll be called Little Boo Boo Sniffles or something equally moronic for the rest of the year. Although, maybe if Dad thinks I'm crying he'll take pity on me . . .

"Edmund," my father says softly. "Your mother agrees with me. Senate is too expensive."

Nope, no pity today. Before I can regroup and reload, a loud cry calls out from behind us:

"Help!"

My dad springs up like a jack-in-the-box and turns his head, eyes shifting toward the alley. For a big guy, the man is seriously quick on his feet.

"Run back to the ice cream shop," he commands in a whisper. "Call the police. I'll meet you there."

He takes off into the alley. *Into the alley.*

What does he always say? Never go into an alley, at any time, for any reason. Lonnrot Family Rule #1: Avoid alleys at all costs. Dangerous places . . .

And now he is gone. Into an alley.

Every muscle in my body fights with my brain. I can't move, can't think, can't do anything. I pray I don't pee right here and now. I grip the slats of the park bench, my fingers curling around the cold wood.

More yelling, this time spiked with my dad's deep voice. His shouts jolt me out of my stupidity, because next thing I know my body has thrown itself behind the bench, crouched down low.

Same stupidity, different location.

Loud men's voices, and now scuffling noises. I flatten my stomach against the pavement, cramming myself under the bench. The cement scrapes at my bare knees. Quite the hero. For once I am psyched to be small.

What do I do? What do I do?

Blend in to your surroundings, soldier! My friend Jonah's voice shrieks silently in my head. He's obsessed with military stuff. Quickly I take off my red cap. Without it, maybe I can pass for a blob of garbage; my black winter coat looks like a trash bag, right?

This is the worst hiding place ever. I might as well just lie across the open sidewalk. There are no bushes, no newspaper kiosks, *nothing* to hide behind. Should I try to flag down a passing car? It's New York City—no one's going to stop unless it's a cab. Plus I'm too chicken to move.

I strain to hear what's happening. The only sounds are my pulse hammering in my ears, the rustling fabric of my jacket against the gritty stone, and the *whoosh* of a few cars passing by, their wheels barely visible from my strange hideout. No birds, no dogs, no people. Just machinery and alley brawls in this weather.

Must do something.

I try to fish my cell phone out of the mountain of down quilting I'm tangled in. Finally a chance to call 9-1-1!

Bumbling the phone with icy fingers, I watch helplessly as it clatters away from me on the cement. Terrific.

Assess your situation! Work with what you have! More of Jonah's combat tactics tick through my mind. Okay, assessing . . . assessing . . . I am wearing shorts and lying on a sidewalk in January. My cell phone is out of reach. I smell gum.

A new wave of fear tightens my lungs as a man comes sprinting out of the alley and whizzing by my park bench. His long black hair and weird, spindly goatee fly back in the breeze as he books out of there. He's holding a bloody knife in his hand, too distracted to notice the kid sprawled out on the ground.

Click goes the camera in my mind.

A bloody knife?

My dad bolts out of the alley and arrives back at the bench, winded. My eyes strain to assess any damage through the slats of wood. Blood stains on his coat? Fingers grasping his side in agony? Just heavy breathing. He hunches over, hands on his knees, and slows his panting. I want to say something, tell him I'm glad he's okay, but my mouth won't open. His shoes start to turn in the direction of the ice cream place, then shuffle and stop, as if he's confused.

"I thought I told you to go to the ice cream shop."

I was right. Lamest hiding spot ever.

"Sorry, Dad," I say as I squeeze out of my crawl-space, limbs finally able to move under the protection of his faint winter shadow. "My legs didn't work."

He hugs me and squats down, sliding my hat back on and staring straight into my face. "Did you get a good look at the guy?" he asks.

I nod and he smiles.

"That's my boy. Let's go call the police."

The man from the alley didn't see me, but I sure saw him. Unlucky for him, very lucky for everyone else.

You see, I have a photographic memory.

And *that* will be very interesting to the police when they arrive.

Chapter 2

FIRST PORTRAIT

—

"Can you spell your last name for me?"

The lady at the police station clacks away on her keyboard as she questions me. She's got wire-rimmed glasses and a pleasant voice. When we arrived, she gave me a soda to ease my nerves. I guess sugar does that in these situations.

"L-O-N-N-R-O-T."

People always ask how to spell my name. It's European and looks pretty unusual, but it's easy to pronounce: Lawn-rot. Some family down south owned my ancestors back in the slave days, and the name stuck.

"And Edmund is your son?" she asks my father with a smile, polite like it's obvious and yet . . . there's doubt. I share my dad's dark skin and need for thick glasses, but the genetics end there. He is a mammoth, and I am a chipmunk.

"That is correct."

"Sir, we'd like to take your statement soon, but your son is a priority due to his—"

"Photographic mind, yes," my father replies, beaming with pride. Oh brother, here we go.

Before he can get to talking about how I'm enrolled in a school for gifted kids, the policewoman vanishes and reappears with an older man whose big fuzzy blond mustache makes him look like Sherlock Holmes. But instead of a pipe, he pulls out a fancy coal pencil and a sketchpad.

"Edmund, this is Mr. Wright. He's a sketch artist, and will be drawing the man you saw. Just describe him the best you can." She gestures to an empty desk with two seats. "Let me know if you need anything."

Mr. Wright shakes my hand and sits, motioning for me to follow. His blue eyes crinkle at the corners. "You can call me Phil," he says. "Let's start with any striking details you remember, okay? And then we'll think about the shape of his face, his eyes, if his nose was long . . . things like that. Sound good to you?"

I nod, picturing the man's face in my head. My dad is distracted, talking to another cop a few feet away, which is just as well or he might seriously interfere with this process.

We work on the picture for twenty minutes. I describe, Phil draws.

"How's this?" Phil asks. He leans forward, sliding the picture across the table. In this close proximity, I become painfully aware of the tufts of hair growing out of his ears and nose.

"The eyes aren't quite right," I reply. "They were a different shape, and farther apart. It's like he was Chinese, but not. More almond-shaped, I guess."

Phil nods and pensively begins to erase some markings. I don't have the heart to tell him that none of it looks right. The beard is too full, the hair not stringy enough. And don't even get me started on the nose and forehead.

I fiddle with a pen and zone out as he labors away. I can hear what my dad is saying two desks over:

"There were two men fighting. I pulled them off each other. One was clearly hurt. Knife wound, I think. He was probably the one who yelled for help. He was clean-shaven, Caucasian, and completely bald. A young guy. Shaved his head so it shined. Not in a skinhead way, though. He seemed pretty preppy to me. Probably one of those guys who's prematurely bald so he decided to just shave it all off."

My dad starts to pontificate about the guy's background, but the cop gently steers him back to the task at hand. My father could talk all night if they let him.

"All right. Well, the bald, wounded man took off running once I separated them. An extremely tall fellow. I'm a big guy and he had some inches on me. Six foot six at least. Very thin. And then there was the man with the long hair and beard, the one my son saw."

My dad moves his head in my direction when he mentions me. Quickly I pretend to be engrossed in what Phil is doing. Or not doing, which is the case. He has completely botched my description of the eyes, going from bad to worse.

"Anyway, the guy with the beard . . . I've decided his name is Marco, by the way. He sort of looked like an Asian Marco Polo." My dad chuckles at his joke. No one else laughs.

Clearing his throat, he continues: "Marco had a knife in his hand, so I put my fists up, ready to punch. I've taken self-defense classes. He saw me preparing to defend myself, and I probably outweighed him by a hundred pounds, so he ran. I chased after him but then I saw my son under the bench, so I stopped."

I'm pretty sure my dad stopped because he hasn't

jogged for twenty years, let alone sprinted, but I stay quiet and let him keep his dignity.

"How about this?" Phil's voice interrupts my thoughts.

"The mustache had a different shape, thinner in this area," I say, grabbing a pencil and making a few line adjustments on the paper.

Phil gasps as if I just marked up an original Picasso.

He snatches the sketchpad back, and his arm tenses as he erases the lines in angry, jerking bursts. I sigh. We're going to be here all night.

By the sixth round of show-and-tell, Phil is beyond annoyed, a grimace twisting his once friendly mouth. I try to be helpful:

"Sir, I'm pretty good at drawing. Do you mind if I try? In addition to your picture, I mean. For backup." Backup? Is that even the right word in this situation?

"Kid, this is a professional job, not some project for school."

I paste on my most charming smile. "Please, I won't get in the way. I think it could be helpful. I won an art contest last year. Your picture is great and all . . . It's just to have a different perspective."

He eyes me for a moment, his fuzzy mustache

twitching like an irritated caterpillar. "Fine. Let's see what you can do."

I know a dare when I hear one. He slaps a fresh sheet of paper down on the table and walks away chuckling as if he's humoring the silly boy with his silly art ideas. I notice he takes his writing instrument with him. No cool police sketching coal for me.

I pick up a pencil from the desk and quickly start to sketch, imagining I'm in art class. If I think about how the man I'm drawing had a knife and could have left me fatherless, I get rattled. So I pretend he's just a long-lost weirdo relative who I have to draw for my grandma's birthday gift. So what if he's white and has bizarre facial hair? He's adopted. Marco Lonnrot. Every family has one.

I grip my pencil from the side to make quick, fluid strokes. I sketch an oval head, centering the eyes, nose and mouth. Marco's mouth was wider than normal, his cheekbones protruding. I measure the proportions mentally, his face as clear in my mind as if he were standing in front of me.

Phil walks by and snickers. The picture looks weird with its rough scribbles and geometric outlines, but I'm not done yet. *Darn you and your fancy charcoal, Phil.*

I speed up, loosening my shoulder and making big sweeping motions on the paper.

Eyes were big but angled at the corners. Wisps of hair flowing from his chin. Hair on head stringy, straggling down to his shoulders. Shading behind the eyes so they don't pop from the paper. Shade and erase. Shade and erase. I wish I had charcoal. Much easier to work with.

A group of people has gathered behind my shoulder, whispering. I try to ignore them.

"Hey, Chief! Come take a look at this," a guy calls out from my right.

An older man in a sharp navy blue uniform walks over, the top of his left shoulder lined with four gold stars. His weather-worn face is stern but his eyes curious.

The chief of police is watching you! Don't mess this up! Swallowing my nerves, I put final touches on everything with crisper lines. One more rub of the eraser . . . proportions correct, photograph complete. Welcome to the room, Marco.

Someone whistles; a couple people clap.

I can tell my father is about to explode with pride as several onlookers compliment him on his gifted geek son. I sit back and admire my work. Not my

MARCO

best, but not bad, under the circumstances. It took about ten minutes.

Phil examines my drawing for a moment, then gazes down at his own, a warped, hollow imitation of the real thing.

"Beginner's luck," he snaps. He turns on his heel and stalks away, head held high as if he has much more important places to be. I overhear the nice cop lady say, "Don't worry, Phil. You're still the best artist in the precinct. In the whole city, in fact."

I don't think there's one person in the room who believes that, considering the way they are all looking at me now.

Sorry, Phil.

Chapter 3

GLORY

January 14

"That is totally Alamo," whispers Jonah during math class the next morning. I decided to tell him what happened first, before the story breaks and I get swarmed by the rest of the sixth grade. Privileges of the best friend.

"Yeah. Totally Alamo," I agree, not actually knowing what he's talking about. Something to do with battle strategy.

I can track the years of my life with Jonah's military obsessions. They usually coincide with whatever language we're studying. We learn a different language each year, and the theory is that by seventh grade we'll be able to make an "educated decision" about what we'd like to study for good. As if my seventh grade mind can predict that I'll enjoy French at age eighteen. But the school stands by their system.

JONAH

Anyway, two years ago when we studied German, Jonah fixated on the Red Baron and World War I. (I use the term "studied" loosely. More on that in a moment.) Last year, it was Napoleon (French class). And don't even get me started on the third grade and his whole *Braveheart* William Wallace mania involving blue paint and a whole lot of Scottish plaid. Those guys don't wear anything under their kilts, you know.

This year it's Spanish, and the Alamo, Mexico, Texas, and whoever else was involved in that mess.

If I ask Jonah what he means about the Alamo, he'll derail into a long lecture. I need to keep him on track so I can talk about my near-death ice cream experience.

He leans closer, body rocking in his chair, sending tremors my way like a miniature earthquake. His red curly hair bounces as a wild gleam shines in his blue eyes. This is his "active boy" look, a term that my mother coined for him. It's her polite way of saying Jonah is never allowed near her china cabinet unsupervised again.

"So can I tell people?" he asks.

"Yeah, but—"

"Boys! What are you doing?" Mrs. Reed interrupts our discussion. I guess it's pretty obvious from where she's standing that we're not working on the graphing problem.

"Sorry, Mrs. Reed!" Jonah calls out in a loud voice. "Edmund was just telling me an über-cool story about a robbery and having to go to the cops' last night. He was almost killed!"

I die of embarrassment.

The class explodes with excited questions and Mrs. Reed officially loses control of the children. Only for a moment, though.

"Everyone, settle down. I am aware of what happened to Edmund last night. His mother sent in a note. I didn't realize he was in such mortal peril . . ." She inspects me over her glasses. How can adults do sarcasm with their eyes? Do they go to school for it? Maybe they teach it in college.

"Jonah, may I remind you that we do not use the word *über* in this classroom. Edmund, would you care to share your story with us since we *clearly* will not be able to concentrate until you do? And without exaggeration, please?"

Thanks a lot, Jonah. I frown at his dumb freckly face. His foot is tapping as he grins a toothy smile at me. I am seriously going to kill him later.

During my timid explanation, I carefully avoid the

word *über* at all costs. Mrs. Reed is nice, but she has a temper when we abuse her good graces.

Two years ago we had an unusual German teacher, Frau Faberstein, who had some questionable theories on education. She claimed that eating German food would turn us into German speakers, as would singing mindless children's songs, even if we didn't understand what the words meant. So our fat levels spiked from the pounds of bratwurst sausage and Emmentaler cheese she stuffed into us, and we gained a finer appreciation for such ditties as *"Funkel, funkel, kleiner Stern."* She was fired later that year.

The only thing anyone got out of the class was the word *über* (pronounced *oober*), which means "very." Everything became "über-this" and "über-that," kind of like our class code. I guess we über-abused it, because the teachers joined forces and über-banned it from their classrooms. You'd think they'd want us to practice our new language. Geez.

As I finish my knife-in-alleyway story, I can tell that my coolness level (or "street cred" as my uncle Jay calls it) has just shot up a few points, judging from the awestruck faces in the classroom. Even Jenny Miller, the shiest and prettiest girl in our class, is smiling at me.

"So what happened to your ice cream cone?" blurts out Milton Edwards.

"Cone?" Jonah roars. "Who cares about the stupid ice cream cone? We're talking *attack* here, Milton. *Life and death*. Edmund employed camouflage techniques to *stay alive*. Quick wits and clever disguise! Cones!" he snorts, as if the question is the most ridiculous one he's ever heard.

"Thank you, boys," Mrs. Reed says firmly, signaling the End of the Discussion.

And my two minutes of sixth grade glory are over.

Chapter 4

MR. PEE

———

No one lets me eat at lunch. They keep bugging me with questions like *Did the guy have a machete? Did the cops really clap for you at the station? Was your Dad stabbed? Did he lose a finger? Did you lose a finger?*

At first it's fun but after a while the questions grow stupider and stupider and now I'm starving.

By art class my cool status has waned and things are back to normal. Jonah and I are sitting side by side on tall stools, canvases resting on easels in front of us. The classroom is plastered with pictures of lakes and forests and mountains for this week's assignment: "idyllic landscapes."

"So what else is wrong with you?" Jonah asks, his face crinkled up as he scrutinizes me.

"Nothing. I'm hungry is all," I say, frowning at the tree I'm painting. Something weird is going on with the leaves. I adjust the edge of my canvas, which is crooked against the rickety wooden easel. The leaves still look weird.

"Are you suffering from post-traumatic stress disorder?" he presses, rearranging his paintbrushes for the millionth time and tapping his foot in perfect rhythm. Tap-tap-tap, pause-pause-pause.

"No, it's nothing."

Jonah is too good when it comes to reading me. This morning at home, I found an informational packet about the local middle school resting on my desk, and promptly threw it in the trash. I'm trying to force the whole changing-schools situation out of my mind. I *will* find a solution. Maybe Jonah will rob a bank for me. He could definitely mastermind it.

"So you rode in a cop car?" he says. "What was it like? Did you feel like a criminal?"

Tap-tap-tap, pause-pause-pause.

I shrug. "It was kind of boring. Like a taxi crossed with a jail. No door handles, and a big metal barrier separating us from the cops. All of the cool stuff was up front. I could barely see it."

I give up on the tree and start to work on a pond,

dipping my brush into the paint set that rests between us on a small table.

"Huh," Jonah replies, fussing with his brushes again. He hasn't made very much progress on his canvas. Just a vertical brown line for a tree and a horizontal gray squiggle that might be a cloud. Or a sickly flying worm.

Tap-tap-tap, pause-pause-pause.

Jonah has OCD, or "obsessive-compulsive disorder" in adult-speak, which basically means that he's constantly rearranging everything into neat and orderly categories. He taps on stuff a lot, has a hard time controlling his impulses (which lands him in the principal's office on occasion), and generally avoids any and all cracks on the ground when he's walking. He's also über-brilliant and makes me snort milk out my nose at lunch at least once a week from laughing so hard. And my bedroom at home is very tidy and organized thanks to his weekend visits.

"Hey, Puddles, watch out!" grunts a beastly voice behind us. A fat hand shoves Jonah on the shoulder, hard, knocking him into our tray of paints.

Robin Christopher.

Robin picks on Jonah a lot and I'm not sure why.

ROBIN CHRISTOPHER

As Jonah's best friend I know I'm obligated to stand up for him, but Robin Christopher is huge, so I usually just stand there showering evil thoughts upon him and feeling like a puny idiot.

"Ha! Ha! Ha!" His Neanderthal laugh follows him to the other side of the room.

Nobody understands what Robin's problem is. The running theory is that he's messed up because his name is backwards; it should be Christopher Robin, the name of that nice British boy from the Winnie-the-Pooh stories. Instead it's twisted around, making him the opposite of the storybook character.

Robin calls Jonah "Puddles" and is trying to get other kids to do it, but no one likes Robin so they blow him off. The name Puddles comes from an ill-fated day with an incident involving me, Jonah, Wendy Friml, and our science teacher, Mr. Patterson. The only one who got stuck with a nickname after that one was the teacher.

Although my actions triggered The Incident, I swear that I was an innocent bystander in the whole thing:

We were in the lunch line and I went to grab a red apple. I turned too quickly and grabbed Wendy Friml's elbow by mistake. (In my defense, she was wearing a red, fuzzy sweater and kind of looked like an apple.) Wendy screamed and I jumped out of my skin, dropping my tray in the process. Then the girls behind Wendy screamed, because that's what girls do, more trays and food were dropped, and Jonah laughed so hard that he literally peed his pants right then and there. I'm talking down his leg, mess on the floor.

Mr. Patterson came over to see what was going on and slipped on a warm yellow puddle, crashing down in a tumble of science-teacher plaid and khaki. Both he and Jonah had to change their clothes. So far it's been the high and low points of sixth grade.

Poor Mr. Patterson. At the beginning of the school year he had said, "Call me Mr. P," but now of course when we say "Mr. P" it sounds like "Mr. Pee" because, well, he was covered in Jonah's pee two months ago, and people start to giggle. A few days after it happened he announced, "I'd prefer to be called Mr. Patterson from now on." Which really just made it worse.

Jonah is tapping on his stool harder and faster, staring at the mess that Robin Christopher left in his wake. The paints that were neatly organized in rows between us are now smeared in a messy rainbow. Jonah's mouth puckers up and I know he's upset, so in a panic, I lie.

"Hey, I asked the officer if sometime I could bring my buddy down to sit in the front of a cop car and check it out, you know, sort of like an educational tour, and he said yes. So let's call him next week."

Jonah lights up and starts planning out a way to hijack a cop car while making it look like an innocent mistake.

I know lying is wrong, but how bad can it be when it makes your best friend smile and forget all about the brute who just pushed him around?

That night I lie awake thinking, staring at the glow-in-the-dark stars on my ceiling, flipping through the pictures in my mind methodically, one at a time. Snapshots of a time sequence from yesterday.

I don't think about Mr. Pee or Jonah or bullies or cute Jenny Miller or even my moment of artistic fame at the police station.

All I can think about (and I curse Milton Edwards until midnight for planting this in my brain):

What the heck *did* happen to my ice cream cone?

Chapter 5

MAKE THE CALL

January 21

The phone call comes at four thirty in the afternoon on Friday, a week later. Mom and I are on the couch in our living room, watching a mindless movie about robots.

Usually I don't pay attention to my mother's phone conversations, especially the business ones: *blah blah blah, mortgage rates, blah blah blah, property on Horicon Street.* She's a real estate agent.

But this call is different. She stands and nervously paces into the kitchen, closing the swinging door behind her.

I try to follow. Sadie, our cat-who-may-be-an-evil-overlord-in-disguise, heads me off. Leaping in front of the kitchen door, she arches her back in a ripple of fur and hisses.

Sadie is the ugliest cat I have ever seen. She has

white, fluffy hair that looks like it's been shocked with electricity in all the wrong places, unpleasant green eyes, and a flat face, as if someone dropped an iron on her when she was little. A face only my parents love.

SADIE

I nudge her gently with my hand, a signal to move or be moved. She claws my arm. "Ow!" I shout, hopping back and rubbing the scratched skin. The movement is enough to scare her off. She runs into my father's office, mewing pathetic cries as if *I'm* the one who just caused *her* physical pain. I hear my dad make some cooing baby noises at her. Like I said: pure evil.

Mom shoots me a glare as I barge into the kitchen and prop myself up on the counter. "Yes, Chief Williams," she says into the phone, "my husband mentioned you. We're doing well, thank you. What's that? Today? Well, it's almost dinnertime. Hmm, I see. All right, tomorrow morning it is. Yes. See you then."

She hangs up. "Edmund, when I come into the kitchen, it means it's a private conversation. You know that." She smooths her hair off her forehead the way she does when she's upset, and leaves without further comment.

"The police called? What did they want? Are we going in again? What's going on?" I'm a spazzy Chihuahua jumping out the door after her.

Ignoring me, she sits down on the edge of the couch, her back rigid. "Who was on the phone?"

Dad asks, watching her from the office doorway with curious eyes, no doubt smelling the scent of Mom Angst as it drifts through the room.

"Chief Williams," she replies. "The police want to see you again. Tomorrow at ten. Both of you. All of us."

My father strides across the carpet to join her on the couch. I stay by the wall, hoping that if they forget I'm in the room, they'll speak more freely.

"Probably caught the guy and want us to identify him," Dad says.

Mom shrugs and chews on her lower lip. She's still angry that my father went down the alley in the first place. Of course, he left out most of the details about the fight, making it sound as if he didn't use physical contact to separate the two men, as if his mere presence parted them the way Moses parted the sea. She didn't buy the story last week and she doesn't now. She squints at both of us with a weird expression of worry and suspicion, wrinkling her nose and crinkling her eyebrows like she may need to use the bathroom in a hurry.

Dad puts a gentle arm around her shoulders. "Don't worry, my beautiful Nile rose. It's just standard procedure. If you witness a crime, you have to answer a lot of questions. Say, do they grow roses in Egypt? I'll have to look it up." He grabs his laptop from the coffee table and settles in to the cushion beside her for an hour of geeking out on North African flora and fauna. Mom takes the bait and rests her head on his shoulder, forgetting momentarily about the phone call.

I roll my eyes and start down the hallway to my bedroom.

Mom and Dad did a special genetic testing thing last year to discover their long-lost African ancestry. It's all the rage in their group of friends. Dad's genes were mostly linked to the area in Nigeria where the Hausa tribes live, while Mom's seemed to match the northern parts of Africa, Egypt especially. I guess that explains the coffee-with-cream skin she's got.

Anyway, ever since the test results came back it's been Egyptian-goddess-this and Hausa-warrior-that and things have reached an extreme barf level around here.

Chapter 6

THE TEST

January 22

"Hello, Mr. Lonnrot. Edmund." Chief Williams greets us by the precinct's elevator the next morning. He's not wearing his navy blue uniform today, but is still formal in a starched white shirt and blue tie. "And where is your lovely wife?"

"She had to show apartments this morning," my dad replies. "Real estate business."

I'm relieved that my mother isn't here, 'cause I'm pretty sure she'd be a major wet blanket. She gave us both an extra-big hairy eyeball as we were leaving this morning, as if *we* were the ones pulling knives out in alleyways.

The chief escorts us up to the third floor and into his office, where we take a seat on a soft, comfortable couch. The room is spacious, with dark wood and important-looking photographs hanging on the walls. Also a plaque from 9/11. Clearly Chief Williams has seen a lot of action.

He sits across from us in a leather chair, twisting a ring on his finger and asking us dumb questions about our health. He has silvery hair and a perma-tan that offsets his shiny white teeth, except the chief doesn't smile much. Probably too busy and stressed with such an important job.

He seems nervous, which is strange. Surely my father and I do not constitute a high-pressure situation. After fiddling with a pen and commenting on the weather, he gets to the point:

"I'll just lay it out there for you. We've never done this before. It's inconceivable. But so is your son's talent. The picture he drew . . . well, let's just say it was like a photograph. A perfect match to a mug shot that we have from a few years back. Never seen anything like it in my thirty-two years on the force. We have a business proposal for you. For Edmund, actually. If you would be interested."

"What?" My dad is too stunned to say anything more intelligent.

Chief Williams nods in understanding. "It is an unusual situation, isn't it? The men you saw in the

44

alley—we suspect that they're part of a larger group of thieves. Real professionals. We'd like Edmund to help us catch them. We could use his talents."

Go after professional thieves? Holy cow! But my father is frowning.

The chief holds up a reassuring hand. "There's no chance of bodily harm. It's strictly reconnaissance. A surveillance job at various art museums throughout the city. It's not a violent crime case. Just a potential robbery." He pauses so my dad can digest this information. When Dad doesn't speak (because he's as shocked as I am), the chief continues:

"First, Edmund will have to pass a test, make sure he's as good as we think he is. And then . . . ten hours a week, perhaps? The days can be flexible around your schedules. We'll compensate him for his efforts, of course."

Compensate as in *pay?* As in, I have a job that will help fund Senate Academy? My heart soars and I almost fall out of my chair. It's a miracle.

My father sniffs. "Use the taxpayers' money to pay my son? It doesn't seem right."

Come on, Dad! I scream in my head.

"He'll be doing a civic duty," the chief replies.

"Earning every penny. You can be his chaperone on site, with him at all times. Neither of you will know any details about the case. Minimal risk."

This is *awesome*. Jonah is going to flip. I start to twitch in my seat. A squeak of joy escapes my body.

The chief smiles. "I can see that Edmund is onboard." Leaning closer, he speaks in a low voice to my dad. A sympathetic voice. "Mr. Lonnrot, we understand that you recently lost your job, and that Edmund's school is quite costly. We'd like to help further the education of such a talented young man."

"You lost your job?" I blurt out. "I thought you just lost some hours!"

"I did. I got laid off two days ago. It seems the police have up-to-date information." My dad eyeballs the chief with mild disgust, like the guy has infiltrated his private world. Which he has.

I agree it's a little creepy that the police know everything about our lives, but I don't care. I want in on this deal.

As if reading my father's mind, the chief offers him an apologetic shrug. "We have access to a lot of information. I assure you no further investigation will be conducted in regards to your family."

The loud tick of the NYPD clock fills the office as I await The Decision. I beg my dad with pleading eyes, mouthing *Please* over and over.

He crumbles. "It's not me you have to worry about, Edmund. I will consider this proposal. I think it's an interesting idea. But first you need to pass the chief's test. And then . . . there's Mom."

I don't need to tell you which of the two is going to be more challenging.

I turn to the chief. "Let's have the test. I'm ready."

"All right. And while you work, I'll talk to your father about the details and legality issues. I'm sure he has some safety concerns."

My father nods in agreement, his mustache moving back and forth the way it does when he's gearing up for an intellectual debate. The chief has no idea what he's in for. My dad can *talk*.

Chief Williams leans forward, twirling a pen between his fingers. I can tell he's excited about this; he wants me to succeed. "And now for the test: There were two other people riding in the elevator with us on our way up here this morning. We planted them there. They are officers whom you have never met before, as far as we know. They work upstairs in the

Narcotics Division. If you can . . . conjure them up in that photographic memory of yours and draw accurate sketches of them, then the job is yours."

"There were two extra people in the elevator? I thought there were three," my dad says, trying to be helpful. Rookie.

I close my eyes and think of the elevator. A man and a woman. I focus on their faces, their clothing, even the names on their badges. When I open my eyes, there is worry on the chief's face. Probably thinks I'm not up to the task. I flash him a grin.

"I'll need a sketchpad and that cool coal pencil that Phil was using last week. I'd be happy to draw a picture of Officers Hopkins and McGrady for you."

The pen slips from Chief Williams's hand and falls to the ground when I use their names.

Game on.

Chapter 7

BOVANO

The chief leads us out to the main area, pointing me to a vacant desk where a secretary is setting up paper and charcoal. He and my dad take a stroll, leaving me to my work.

The room is enormous, housing the majority of the officers in the unit. Every available space is lined with desks and bodies either hunched over work or standing and yelling to someone across the way. It's just like in the movies: phones are ringing and people are walking by with papers and coffee, talking about everything from the weather to a hockey game to the junkie they brought in yesterday.

I push my glasses up on my nose and get to work. Showtime. *These are important pictures, Edmund. Senate is on the line.*

Gripping the black stick between my fingers at a slant, I rotate my shoulder and let my arm hang loosely as I draw long, fluid swirls of an oval face. I love charcoal. It's hard yet soft on the paper, and it erases with the touch of a cloth. I can go from light to dark shading with one quick smudge. The black flakes float across the paper like dust; no line is permanent until I force it to be.

I start with the woman, Officer Hopkins. She was attractive, with deep-set eyes, her hair swept across her forehead, the shape of her bangs following the contour of her head. Laugh lines around her mouth. She was serious and looked tired, but at one point on the elevator ride she gave me a soft smile. I draw her that way. I hope they show her the picture. I think she'll like it.

I finish with her after fifteen minutes and check to see if my dad is around. He's chatting with some cops by a water cooler, and they have that look of alarm on their faces. He's probably telling them who invented the water cooler.

I don't have the audience around me like last time. In fact, no one seems to notice me there at all. Still, I can't shake the feeling that I'm being watched. And then I spot him.

A man is staring at me from across the room. He's

sitting in an office with huge windows, but the glass barrier does nothing to shade the gazer beam he has locked on me. It's like he's trying to penetrate my brain.

He's got dark eyes and salt-and-pepper hair, with huge bushy eyebrows to match. Deep creases line his face, evidence of at least a few stressful decades under his belt. He's not so much staring as glaring at me. Displeasure radiates from his scowl and rolls over me like a hot wind. I scan the room to see if there's someone he's sneering at behind me, maybe somebody who owes him money or ran over his dog.

Nope, it's just me.

I ignore him and get to work on the second drawing. *Focus, Edmund!*

The secretary pulls me away while I'm fussing with the final details, telling me I have to meet my contact.

"Isn't Chief Williams my contact?" I ask as she whisks me across the room by my elbow.

She shakes her head and points to the glass office where the grumpy man stands and comes out, a hefty frame revealing itself from behind the office walls.

Figures.

"Edmund, this is Detective Bovano. He'll be handling your potential employment here." The secretary rushes off, leaving me alone. With him.

I try to smile and squeak out a "Hi."

My dad appears out of nowhere, which is a huge relief because it turns out that the detective is a very large man. Not quite as big as my dad, but almost.

Bovano throws a fake smile on as he shakes my father's hand. "Good to meet you, Mr. Lonnrot. I'll be the one handling your special case here. Why don't you look over some of the paperwork we've drawn up for you while I get to know Eddie a little bit?"

"It's Edmund," I correct him. Few things irritate me more than being called Eddie.

He ignores me and hands my dad a stack of papers, showing him to a seat far, far away, then lumbers back, beckoning for me to enter his office. I'm glad the window shades are open because I'm a little scared at the moment, truth be told. Things may go down, and I need witnesses.

Detective Bovano has some cool trophies in his office, one of an eagle in particular, that I check out when we enter.

"Mr. Bovano, what's this award for?" I ask, trying to break the ice. Maybe I misinterpreted the glares.

And if he's my contact, that means we'll be good friends in the end, right? Gruff cop comes to view naïve young boy as the son he never had.

"Do *not* touch anything in here, and it is *Detective* Bovano. Now sit," he barks, pointing to a chair.

So much for breaking the ice.

I sit.

He remains standing, staring out the window. He has quite a pasta/beer belly packed onto his tall body. This man is what my mother would call a tough cookie. Only he's more like a tough loaf of old and angry Italian bread, with too much garlic mixed in.

"Kid, I've been working this office for twenty years, and I've never seen anything like this. It's not right, asking a child to help the police. No offense, Eddie," he says, staring at me now. I liked it better when he was looking out the window.

"Edmund," I say again.

"I've been working on this case for almost three years," he continues, pointing to a wall where papers are hanging up. Mug shots, lists with arrows, and a city map decorate the bulletin board in a colorful collage.

"They want it solved. It involves a lot of money and some big fancy rich folks. People are starting to get desperate, budgets are being cut. Makes the department look bad. Now they think a kid is going to save them. This is not the way to fix it. You probably won't get the job. Nothing is set, so don't get your hopes up. I designed the test for you myself. Impossible to do, I'd wager."

He sounds proud of himself with that statement. I have no idea what to say, because I'm pretty sure I just aced it.

A knock on the door startles us both. The secretary comes in and whispers something in Bovano's ear.

"What? There must be a mistake. I want to see them," he orders. He flicks a glare at me, then shuffles through some papers, pretending to seem busy.

I try not to stare but it's hard to look away. His paunchy cheeks, humorless eyes, and shaggy eyebrows cause him to bear a striking resemblance to a yeti. He's got a much more complicated face to draw than most, with the extra lines set in his skin and the unkempt head of hair. No smooth motions of charcoal for this guy.

The woman returns moments later, holding my drawings.

Bovano inspects them, mouth slightly open in shock.

BOVANO

The pictures are good. I know they're good. He knows they're good. And I know that he knows they're good. Über-good.

Placing the papers down on his desk, he studies me a moment.

"Well, Eddie," he says in a quieter voice. "Looks like you got the job."

I don't even correct him about my name. I am way too happy to care.

Chapter 8

PERFECT FITS

—

Two hours later

For the first time in my life, I really, truly despise my mother.

"Edmund, if you think for one second that I'm going to let you pal around with the police, and be near guns and Tasers and who knows what else, then you are sorely mistaken, young man." She's pacing the living room, hands on her hips in an "I'm listening but not really because I've already made up my mind" kind of posture.

"Mom, it's totally safe! Just ask Dad. I'm not doing fieldwork or anything. It's just surveillance. I have to draw pictures of people walking by. That's it! Dad will be with me the whole time, hanging out. And I get to stay at Senate, pay my own way. Isn't that amazing? Why aren't you proud of me? This is the greatest thing to happen to me, *ever*."

"It's not just a safety issue, Edmund. First of all, I don't know how much time this is going to require. Dad needs to find another job. What if he can't come? And then there's your schoolwork. What if they want you to work evenings? Weekends? You know our rules. You need to dedicate yourself to your studies."

"Mom, it's art. Drawing portraits. I bet I can get extra credit, even! Plus school is easy. I just pretend that the homework is too much so you won't make me do more."

Sometimes I say incredibly stupid things.

She smooths a strand of hair off her forehead. "I'm going to have to think about this, and talk with your father. I'll be honest . . . It's not looking good, sweetie."

I am shaking with anger, ready to vomit on the living room rug. I should, just to spite her. Instead I throw what is to become known in our family history as the Fit of all Fits.

"You OWE me this, Mom. You do. This is something that I really want and I never ask you for anything. Ever. And YOUR cat killed my hamster but you don't see me asking you to get rid of her or telling you what to do, and—"

"What does Sadie have to do with you working for the police?"

"It's all about principles, Mom! And sacrifice. And I think I'm a pretty good son and I never ask for anything, and you're always saying I have a gift and someday I should put it to use for the greater good and this is it! This is my chance! AND YOU OWE ME THIS BECAUSE I'M SHORT AND IT'S YOUR FAULT AND THIS WILL BE GOOD FOR MY SELF-ESTEEM BECAUSE I'M THE SMALLEST PERSON IN MY CLASS ALL BECAUSE OF YOUR LOUSY EGYPTIAN PRINCESS GENES YOU PASSED ON THAT MADE ME SO PUNY!"

"I see," she says, tight-lipped.

I go to bed without dinner. I'm not hungry anyway.

Chapter 9

EDDIE RED

January 23

We're back at the station the next day. For the first time in my life, I have won a battle against my parents. Maybe it was guilt for letting me starve last night, or maybe it was my compelling yet whiny Thanks-a-lot-for-the-minuscule-bone-structure argument. All I know is that I won, and I'm here. I am invincible.

The chief beckons us into his office, sitting stiffly behind his desk. We follow suit. The wooden chairs are hard and uncomfortable and I wish we were back on his plush sofa talking about cool police jobs and money and happy times.

The chief clears his throat. "Edmund, I'm going to be honest with you. There are people in this department who support your involvement, and there are skeptics."

I'm not going to ask which category Detective Bovano falls into.

Where is the chief going with this? Did he change his mind? Is the deal off? Nerves twist my stomach.

"Money," he continues, his voice rising. "It all comes down to money and budgets and who's paying the bill. We've spent too much money on this case already. We're chasing ghosts and time is running out. You're our last chance to crack the case, our final solution before the powers-that-be pull the plug on the whole operation. No pressure, though." He smiles as if to reassure me. I am not reassured.

"Here are my terms." He places a piece of paper on the desk, a document that I assume is my contract. "Help us solve the case, and we'll make an anonymous contribution to Senate Academy next year, with instructions that it's to go toward your tuition. The operation must be kept very hush-hush. If word got out to the press . . ." His voice trails off, and then he clears his throat again. "It's not illegal," he reassures my dad, whose mustache is twitching like crazy, "although it *is* highly unusual."

Stunned silence. Solve the case? This is not what I expected. I thought they were paying for Senate no matter what. My father shifts in his seat, itching to speak. But he stays quiet and lets me take the lead.

"And if . . . if I can't help?" I say, dreading the answer.

Chief Williams shrugs. "We'll pay you for your time. Minimum wage." The unsaid words *And no more Senate* flash in neon letters.

I straighten my spine and shove my glasses up the bridge of my nose. I can do this. I can solve the crime, whatever it is. "All right," I say. "I'm in."

A shadow passes behind us. I turn to see Bovano lurking outside the door like a shark who enjoys feasting on the flesh of human boys. The chief nods to him. "Edmund, you go and get debriefed with Detective Bovano while I have your father sign some papers."

Dad smiles at me as I stand on wobbly legs. Here we go.

Bovano barrels ahead to his office and I'm forced to jog. He eyes me with the same acidic expression from yesterday and plops himself down behind his desk, pointing for me to sit once again in the hot seat.

Our first official meeting about the case. I'm doing it, I'm really doing police work! I smother a smile and focus on what he's saying.

"You will report to me only. You will listen to all of my instructions and follow them without hesitation. You will not ask questions. You will arrive on time . . ."

My excitement fades a bit as he drones on and on. This is not so much a "debriefing" as a massive lecture on rules. I can boil down everything he says into three basic commands:

1. Don't speak.
2. Don't think.
3. Churn out as many pictures as humanly possible. You are a camera. Nothing more.

"I want to know how it works," he announces.

"How what works?" I say, surprised he has asked me a question after ten solid minutes of sermon. Not really a question. More like an order with an answer expected.

"Your photographic mind. I need to know what I'm dealing with. Doesn't seem very normal to me."

"My mind takes pictures. Snapshots of a moment. It's not like I'm a freak or anything," I mutter.

"But how does it work?" he presses. "Do you remember everything you see? Can you recall it at any time? Seems like your mind would be crammed with too much information."

Does he think my brain will explode on the job?

"I remember things in a different way," I explain. "I remember details that other people don't notice . . . people's shoes, their nametags. It's just there in my mind. But I don't store it away forever. I do forget things eventually. I remember better when I know that I need to, when I'm especially focused. Or in stressful situations . . . like that guy from the alley."

Bovano grunts, unimpressed. "I remember details too. Part of being a detective. Doesn't sound much different from my memory."

I stifle a frustrated sigh and try again. "My memories are like a photograph in my mind. I can study the scene, analyze the details as if I'm holding the actual picture in my hand. I can tell you what kind of watch someone is wearing even if I didn't specifically focus on the watch when I saw it. As long as it passes before my visual field, it's in."

"What if you aren't focused and you miss the suspect walking by? How do I know you can remember everyone you see? You aren't a machine, you aren't perfect. What if you miss a key clue?"

I shrug. "I guess you'll just have to trust me."

I don't think he's very happy with my answer.

After another excruciating seven minutes and fifty-two seconds, we meet up with my dad in the hallway. Bovano walks us out to the elevator, still instructing along the way:

"You'll receive your official assignment next week after a practice run. You will not tell anyone about this. No friends, no teachers, no relatives besides your parents. Absolute secrecy."

I suspect he's telling me this in front of my dad so that my parents will be extra watchful. And so my father doesn't open his big mouth too.

Dad agrees and shakes his hand. Then we step into the elevator and turn back to face the detective. He puts his hand in the door, blocking it so it can't close.

"We needed a code name for you, because you're

a minor and we need to protect your identity. I've decided to call you Eddie Red."

He smiles like it's a personal joke, and then lets the door go.

I open my mouth, proving once and for all why I am in a school for gifted kids:

"Huh?"

The door closes with a soft *swoosh*.

Chapter 10

FOREIGN CODE

January 24

On Monday at school, I withhold the information for exactly three hours and thirty-eight minutes before telling Jonah what happened. What can I say? He's very persuasive.

Jonah may lack self-control, but he is über-trustworthy, and if I ask him not to tell anyone, then he'll take the secret to his grave. It's a military thing. He prides himself on it.

"What?" he yells, choking on his peanut butter sandwich. We're at lunch in the cafeteria at a corner table, tucked away from the crowds so we can talk in private. Even with Jonah's outburst, no one glances in our direction. They're all used to Jonah and his noise levels.

"That is totally, ÜBER-AWESOME!" he says.

"That's Alamo and Waterloo and Red Baron wrapped into one! Wow!"

I can tell that he's a little bit jealous because this police stuff is right up his alley, but he's cool about it and immediately starts to plan out how he's going to help me with assignments.

I don't tell him about the name Eddie Red. I want to figure out for myself why Bovano chose it, and I know Jonah will crack the code in about a millisecond.

Detective Bovano is clearly messing with my head. He doesn't like me, he thinks the entire thing is a waste of time, so he's chosen an undercover name that makes fun of me, I'm sure of it. If only I knew what it meant.

Eddie I get. I told him to call me Edmund, so clearly he's flexing his cop muscles and letting me know that he'll call me whatever he wants.

But Red? What is that all about? Why not call me something awesome, like *Eddie X* because my middle name is Xavier?

"Let's go," Jonah says, crumpling up his brown paper bag and tossing it into the trash. "I have to get my Spanish book."

We return to our lockers in the hall by the science

rooms only to find Jonah's in a complete mess, the orderly stacks of books and papers now in a scattered heap on the floor. His picture of the Red Baron is ripped, and his jacket is missing. We find it later in the art classroom with some paint on it.

Robin Christopher strikes again.

The school doesn't let us put actual locks on our lockers. We operate on an honor code to respect one another's belongings. Someone forgot to mention that to Captain Meathead.

Jonah refuses to tell the teachers about the bullying. I guess he's planning some sort of tactical revenge, but if you ask me, he's just scared. I am too, but we need to do something about it. It's getting worse.

Spanish class. Time to zone out. I wonder if the police could help me with the Robin situation. Maybe Bovano could arrest him for bullying, throw him in jail for the night and scare him into good behavior. Who am I kidding? They'd probably join evil forces and take over the school.

Back to *Red* . . . Is it because I was wearing a red hat when I first went into the station, that day of the ill-fated ice cream cone? That would be totally lame.

Is it because Jonah's hair is red and they know who my friends are? Too creepy.

Sadie's cat collar is red. That would be an ironic twist.

Is it mocking the superheroes somehow? Does Detective Bovano think that since I'm a kid, I enjoy wearing red capes and pretending to fly? I don't.

The name has to be making fun of me somehow. The man does not like me. Maybe I'm overthinking it.

"Edmund! Question seven," Jonah hisses. He kicks my chair from the seat behind me.

"Uh," I say, searching my Spanish workbook while my cheeks heat with embarrassment. "The answer is *ocho?*"

"Muy bien, Edmundo," the teacher replies, writing my answer on the board and moving on to torture someone else. Two aisles over, Jenny Miller catches my eye and smiles. I almost pass out.

I have always thought Jenny Miller is nice, but lately when I look at her there's a weird tightening in my chest. What is that? Love? When you can't breathe and may throw up everywhere? Doesn't sound very romantic to me. Just really messy and life-threatening.

Jenny has pretty blue eyes and strawberry blond hair, and she never speaks, but sometimes she smiles at me, which wigs me out completely. She floats instead of walks, and seems to be completely unaware of her beauty. She's not like the rest of the girls in my class, who were all abducted by aliens last year and came back wearing weird eye makeup and speaking only in giggles.

Jenny Miller is almost perfect, but there's one big problem: she has Happy Kat Cat *everything*. Backpack, shoes, pencils, and a lunch box with matching thermos, to name a few. And I just don't fully trust someone who celebrates cats to that extreme level.

Eddie Red . . . Eddie Red.

I think of the initials: ER. Emergency room? Is that where I'll be going if I mess this up? A subtle threat from the thug cop?

Nothing fits. I can't figure it out.

So much for gifted.

After dinner I can't take it anymore. Time to call in some parental assistance. My dad is, after all, a walking encyclopedia.

"Dad, where does our last name come from?" I figure I'll start with the basics and move on from there.

"It's German. You know that. Back from the slave days. A German family owned our ancestors in Virginia." He's distracted, snuggling with my mom on the couch. This is usually when I exit, but I need answers.

"But what does it mean?"

"I have no idea. You should Google it. And when you do, check out pictures of Nefertiti. The most beautiful Egyptian queen to ever rule. Mom looks just like her. Just look at that brow! That regal nose!"

My mom giggles and leans over to kiss him, whispering something about her strong Nigerian king.

Yuck.

I will admit that my mom is quite pretty. Beautiful, even. She has big brown eyes and sculpted high cheekbones, lips that are heart-shaped and full, and skin as smooth as caramel. Our art teacher is so smitten that he is forever trying to convince her to model for his adult studio classes. I think he has some sketchy posing in mind even though he hasn't come out and said it. Over my dead, scrawny body. Creeper.

I'm hoping that some of those beauty genes kick in during puberty for me, because so far my dad has given me nothing to work with.

Only recently did I figure out how a bookworm like my dad landed a babe like Mom: girls dig muscles. If you're an über-nerd but you're big, somehow it cancels out. I don't care what my pediatrician says. Size matters.

I wander out of the living room and down the hall, obsessing over the name Lonnrot, picking it apart in my brain. Lonn . . . rot. Lonn . . . rot. I stop next to the three steps that lead to my room. I live "upstairs" in our two-bedroom apartment.

My foot hangs suspended midstep. German lessons from two years ago crash over me, along with the pleasant memory of Emmentaler cheese.

"Eureka!" I yell, running up the three steps and jumping back down. "*Rot* means 'red' in German! *Rot* means 'red' in German!"

I fly up and down the steps a few more times. Sadie hisses from somewhere in the apartment.

Eddie Red. Now one of the coolest names they could have given me. A foreign spy name. A German, über-sophisticated undercover agent name that would make even James Bond jealous.

I prepare to crawl into bed and sleep soundly, relieved at finally cracking the code. A good night's sleep is coming my way.

EDDIE RED, ÜBER-COOL SPY.

But a thought plagues me.

Maybe Detective Bovano isn't such a dumb guy after all. Obviously he's taken German classes. What else has he studied?

Maybe he knows ten languages and could work at the CIA if he wanted to. Maybe he *does* work at the CIA. Maybe he's a foreign spy himself, posing as a cop in the city, waiting to take over the world.

Maybe (and the thought makes me shiver under my heavy blankets) — maybe he is über-smart. Brilliant, even.

For some reason, it's unsettling.

Chapter 11

THE IPODICU

January 26

My first day on the job! Earpiece in, sleeve microphone on. I am connected, synchronized, ready.

Armed with . . . an iPod.

"Son, there is no way on God's green earth that we are going to give you a weapon!" Detective Bovano bellowed at me in his office this morning when I asked him about the possibilities. I thought a nice jackknife or dagger on my hip could be pretty useful.

"What about a Taser?" I said after he shot down the sharp blades idea. "Don't I need protection?" I tried to persuade him with a hopeful and winning smile. A smile that even my mom can't say no to.

Detective Bovano is not my mother.

He started to laugh, jowls shaking like Jell-O. "I'm gonna give an eleven-year-old a piece? That's funny. That's hilarious. No way, kid. You're a tourist. An artist. You're in, you observe, you're out. You watch them, we'll watch you. It's that simple."

End of discussion.

So they gave me an iPod. Except it isn't for music. I'm plugged in like I'm listening to a song, but there's no music and the screen is blank. Its face actually contains a camera and a tiny microphone, recording me and my surroundings while I do my thing. An ear bud sits in my ear in case I need instructions. And every twenty minutes I'm supposed to whisper "All clear" into my sleeve, but pretend to be wiping my nose or scratching my chin.

The police are parked in a van just outside the museum, monitoring *everything*.

The iPod is more like an "i-Pod-I-see-you," or in text messaging, "iPod-I-C-U." I've decided to call it an IPODICU, pronounced *iPod-eh-Q*. I'm going to work on patenting the name. Detective Bovano was not impressed when I mentioned it to him on the car ride over, throwing a scowl and a grumble my way. I think he's warming to me.

They send me to Museum Mile.

Also known as Fifth Avenue, it's the chunk of road that runs along Central Park East. It doesn't seem like anything special as you approach: gray buildings mirroring the grassy hills of the park, a busy New York street like any other. Suddenly you stumble onto the steps of the enormous Metropolitan Museum of Art. And then the Guggenheim. The Frick (not a swear word, but a European art museum). The Whitney. World-famous giants on their own, together they are an impressive collection. Housing around eleven museums total, Museum Mile is an art lover's dream. And a thief's.

The museums have state-of-the-art security systems, complete with thermal monitoring, recorded surveillance, and facial recognition software. But Bovano said the computers keep making false positives, errors that are costly and time-consuming. And the thieves we're hunting are known to drastically change their appearances with high-tech disguises and even plastic surgery. Which is where I come in.

Because of my photographic memory, I'm kind of like a supercomputer, a human data system that can reason and think, as well as churn through information at top speed. The cops believe I'll be able to see through a clever disguise, to look beyond a shortened nose or a new jaw line, compare the face to a photo in my mind, and see the perp for who he or she really is.

Let's hope they're right.

I'm at the Met today and although it's just a practice run, I'm nervous, I'll admit it. The police have planted a few cops in disguise from the precinct—I've already seen a guy from Narcotics stroll by in a fake beard—but there's so much going on that I'm having a hard time concentrating.

I have an art canvas propped up on an easel, and I'm trying to copy a painting by Monet that's hanging up on the other side of the room. I dab pinks and blues onto the sheet every few minutes, but I'm not truly focusing because I'm busy surveying the room. I only need to *seem* like I'm an art student. I have a tray of special pastel crayons because they don't let people use real paint inside the museum. Pastels are not my favorite drawing tool. I need some charcoal.

Every once in a while Detective Bovano's face appears on the IPODICU screen, his voice filling my ear, spluttering away and hissing instructions, which causes me to startle and drop my crayons. The museum guard is not too keen on that mess, believe me.

DAD AS TOURIST

Maybe I'm overthinking it, but right now I wish I had Jonah's brain, because something tells me he'd be much more organized about the whole thing.

My father is not helping matters.

He's my chaperone, but somehow *I'm* the one worried about *him*. He's supposed to keep a low profile, but instead looks like a tourist who escaped from an asylum, decked out in ridiculous garb including a Statue of Liberty foam crown and a large camera that hangs from his neck, partially covering his pink (yes, pink!) T-shirt that says I ❤ NEW YORK. I vow to draw a picture of him when I get home, to show my mother what I'm up against.

I try to ignore him. It's not easy. He is sitting on a bench by some impressionist paintings and suddenly gets a case of the giggles. His laughter starts low and rumbling as he hides his face in his hands. Quickly it escalates into loud chuckles that make his belly/camera/pink shirt jiggle and his crown fall off. He's a disaster among masterpieces from the nineteenth century.

And now I am laughing and I just dropped my stupid pastels again and this is simply not working. I walk over to the Monet to pretend to inspect it, mostly so I can compose myself. Leave it to my dad to mess up my first job. The painting is soothing: light-colored streaks of blues, greens, and pinks, water and sky that blend into each other's reflections.

When I turn back, my canvas is gone. Dad's wiping tears from his eyes from laughing so hard, but stops when he sees my confusion. His gaze shifts to the empty spot where the canvas is supposed to be. What just happened?

Bovano's disgusted face comes into view on the IPODICU:

"I think we're done for today. I'll expect your sketches by tomorrow."

I walk back to pack up my stuff, sans canvas. I think someone just stole my artwork not ten feet from where I had my back turned. Some police detective I am.

"Sorry, son," Dad says as we head for the museum exit. "Maybe I'm not cut out for this police . . . er . . . tourist work." His eyes dart around to see if anyone has overheard, as if the second he says the word *police,* men with machine guns are going to drop from the ceiling. No one is within fifty feet of us.

"You see? I've blown our cover already!" he says.

"We're all right, Dad." I grab his arm to drag him

out of there. It's like pulling a marble statue. He's not going to move until he decides to move. Which he finally does.

The sketches that Bovano wants are of the cops in disguise that I saw stroll by today. Five in all. I draw until ten p.m., then climb into bed, pretty pleased with my stack of pictures. Not that Bovano will actually thank me or compliment me on a job well done. After what happened with the stolen canvas and the giggling dad, I'm sure he'll have about fifty negative things to say about my performance. And my father's as well.

Chapter 12

ASSIGNMENT

———

February 1

New topic in art class this week: the self-portrait. Every artist in the history of mankind has done one. Even kindergartners do them. There are millions out there. Faces upon faces, the painter using the model that is most available: himself.

We're set up at large tables in the classroom, each with our own eight-by-eleven-inch mirror. A sketchpad and charcoal lie neatly in front of me. Given my current police job, this should be easy.

"Do my tonsils look big?" Jonah asks, studying his mouth in the mirror. *Tap, tappity, tap, tap.* His fingers drum on the wooden surface between us. He leans over to look into *my* mirror, as if anything's going to be different, and sticks his tongue out like he's at the doctor's office. "Ahhhh." His breath smells like turkey and mustard.

"Jonah. Personal space." I shove him over to his side of the table for the millionth time and grab my mirror, turning my back to him and scooting my chair to the corner of the desk, hopefully out of his reach. Okay, time to sketch. The only thing I see is my enormous glasses. Not so much a self-portrait as a picture of dorkiness. I take them off, squinting at my reflection. Do I have my mother's eyes? Hard to say from my severely nearsighted perspective. They're either buried behind the eyewear or scrunched into slits as I squint to draw them properly.

The rest is pretty straightforward: a small nose, full mouth, decently smooth skin although who knows what will happen there when puberty hits, and roundish cheeks. No startling Egyptian cheekbones for me. My smile is my best feature, or so I'm told, which ironically I get from my dad. Straight teeth and a wide grin. Maybe I'll grow a mustache like him later in life. He did attract my mother, after all.

I decide to do the portrait smiling. I need all the · help I can get.

An eerie feeling sweeps goose bumps across my neck. I realize Jonah's stopped moving. I put my glasses on and glance back at him in alarm, wondering if he's gone into some sort of spastic shock, his brain circuits finally fried. He's watching me with a studious expression. Then he glances around the room to make sure no one's listening.

"How's it going?" he whispers, his blue eyes loaded with meaning. Asking about the case. He's so still, so quiet, that I'm tempted to snap a picture of him on my cell phone to show my parents. *See, Mom? He can be calm when he needs to be.*

I shrug. "The same. No information yet."

"You'll tell me as soon as you know something, right? We have to solve this. You have to come back to Senate next year."

I smile. "Don't worry, we'll figure it out." My voice is strained with forced cheer. We have no information, nothing to help solve the case. I don't even know what the case *is*. Pathetic.

His answering smile is small and sad. I told him last week about how my dad lost his job and now my parents can't afford the school. Worst conversation ever.

"We'll solve it," he agrees. The tapping starts up again. He clears his throat and pulls my mirror into his work area. "Ahhhhh," he says, fogging up the glass. "Are you sure you don't see anything white in my throat? I'm noting some pus in the back left corner. And the tonsils are definitely swollen."

I snatch the mirror from him and remove my glasses, studying my face once more. I position my hand over the paper, ready to draw.

"Hey, why do you keep taking your glasses off?" he asks. "You're blind as a bat. You can't draw without them, Edmund. And your glasses are a part of you. It has to be an *accurate* self-portrait. I'm going to draw my tonsils. Very art nouveau. Are you even listening to me? Edmund! Edmund!"

I roll my eyes and ignore him, but inside I'm relieved. Things are back to normal. At least for today.

February 2

In the end my mother gets the chaperone job.

She has decided that she can read the paper and do Internet business from her iPad on a museum bench while keeping an eye on me, thereby assuring that no one kidnaps me or sets me on fire or whatever other scary scenario is playing out in her mom brain. Plus she likes being in art museums, and my dad needs to start his job search. It's a win-win.

We aren't going to tell her about the stolen canvas, because she would freak out and make me quit. I reviewed the museum tape with Bovano; it appears that some random guy just lifted the canvas and left. The police have decided that it's unimportant and we should just carry on, business as usual.

Detective Bovano is in love with my mother, of course.

"Call me Frank," he says when they first meet at the station.

Frank? Are you kidding me? Even my dad calls him Detective Bovano.

"Nice to meet you, Frank." She smiles at him as he shakes her hand for *waaay* too long. I'm telling you, the woman casts a spell on everyone she meets. Even Jonah is gaga for her, which is just plain gross and clearly against the code of the best friend.

Bovano muscles me into his office by the arm, leaving my mother out in the main area with a cup of tea that he personally fetched for her. I resist rolling my eyes.

"You passed the practice run," he says as he deposits me in the chair in front of his desk. "I have your assignment." He circles the desk and rummages through one of the drawers.

This is it: my assignment! Will he give me folders to read through, or even boxes of all the notes he's made from the past few years of working on the case? I can barely sit still.

He pulls out a small scrap of paper and hands it to me.

"This is it?" I don't mask the annoyance in my tone. The man is infuriating. This entire situation stinks like a bad pastrami sub with rotten cheese.

He gives me a curt nod. "That's it."

I stare at the bleak paragraph, my supposed "debriefing," a minuscule blurb that could have been written by a third-grader:

We are looking for a group of suspected art thieves. They have a leader, a blond man. He and the others have been difficult to catch on surveillance. You need to identify these men, and anyone else suspicious who catches your attention.

"But there's no information here," I say, stating the obvious.

He answers me with a sneer. "What, you expect

me to hand you over the files? Give you the keys to the office? That's all the detail you need," he says, gesturing to the paper in my hand. "Plus these pictures."

He whips out three photos, one of a bald guy who I imagine is the man my father met in the alley, one of a blond man with a trimmed beard, and one of an older man with crazy fluffed-out hair. Bovano holds up the pictures for a split second, then plunks them into a drawer.

"Detective, wait, I—"

"Did you see the photos? Did they *pass through your field of vision*? Yes? Then they're in your brain. According to you."

It's a direct challenge. Why does this man loathe me so much? I nod glumly. They're in there. But I didn't catch the names. Bovano covered up the writing in the lower left-hand corner with his thumb. On purpose, no doubt. "You know this man, of course," he says, pulling out the picture I drew of the guy with the knife. The one my dad calls Marco.

"Yes," I mutter.

"All right, then," Bovano says, standing up. "Those are the most recent pictures we have of the suspects. Your job is to find them. We start tomorrow. Be ready."

THE SUSPECTS

I glance over my shoulder as he ushers me out of the office, focusing on the bulletin board behind his desk where the *real* materials dangle. Names, city maps, possible crime sites . . .

I go home and draw the three men that he showed me, staring at their faces as if they'll speak to me from the page and give me the answers I'm looking for. I need more to go on. How am I supposed to solve this case if I don't have any details?

Chapter 13

FEBRUARY BLUES

———

February

For the next few weeks, they send me to two places: the Neue Galerie and the Jewish Museum, both on Museum Mile. Three, sometimes four times a week, back to the same rooms next to the same stuff.

The Jewish Museum, the Neue.

The Neue, the Jewish Museum.

The Neue (pronounced *noy-ya*) is a collection of Austrian and German art housed in an enormous old mansion with winding staircases. It has a maze of rooms on three separate floors, some filled with famous paintings, some with traveling exhibits, and some with wall-to-wall crystal dishes and vases. The police keep positioning me in the crystal rooms, forcing me to draw goblet upon goblet, which makes my head want to explode. I'm a faces guy, not a dishware artist. Who stands in a kitchen and sketches cups for hours a week? Apparently I do.

The Jewish Museum isn't much better. As the name suggests, it houses All Things Jewish, and although there are interesting paintings and neat exhibits (Curious George, Houdini . . . a lot of cool Jews out there) I am stuck in the collectibles room, where people send in their antiques and everybody *ooh*s and *aah*s. Menorahs are more interesting to draw, with their swooping lines and intricate ornamentation, but after the fiftieth one, I'm losing my mind.

Jonah thinks it's a riot and claims I'll be more Jewish than he is by the end of the month.

I am baffled as to what the police are doing. All this time and money to spy on furniture? Who's going to steal this stuff? I know I sound like my dad, but I'm beginning to believe that the taxpayers' money is being wasted. And honestly, between you and me, who cares? You want the cup? Take it. There are a lot more out there.

I hate to say it, but this is turning into the most boring job ever. Not that I have much to compare it to since it's my *only* job ever. The clock is ticking, I haven't seen any action, and I'm sick of drawing faces, cups, and menorahs, which stinks because I used to love drawing. I added up the hours I've worked so far, multiplied it by minimum wage, and came up with $326.25. I think Senate costs a little bit more.

To top it off, school is tedious because the snow is brown and hard outside and it's way too cold to go out and attempt to kick a ball or shoot hoops. We'd break our ankles on the ice or get frostbite from the wind for sure. So instead we're trapped inside doing puzzles or reading comics while Jonah slowly drives us insane by motoring his mouth at mach ten. That kid needs to be run outside like a colt.

February 26

Speaking of Jonah, he calls on Saturday night. I press pause on the DVD player and pick up the phone. "Hey," I say.

"I'm bored," he says. "What are you doing?"

I sigh and stretch my neck. I've been sitting in the same position for hours. "The usual."

Bovano came up with the brilliant idea of having me watch surveillance recordings of the museums, specifically times when there are extra big crowds and thieves might be hiding in the masses. So now I get to watch black-and-white footage of the cups and me-norahs from the comfort of my own living room. It's as fun as it sounds.

"Can I come over?" he asks. "Maybe I could help."

"Uh . . ." He'll be way too distracting. As it is, I can hear a weird hollow noise in the background, like he's tapping on a bass drum with a pencil. His parents bought him a drum set two years ago to "channel his energy." They've both developed nervous twitches ever since, and startle at loud noises like bomb survivors.

"My parents aren't home" is my lame excuse. I look at the stack of disks Bovano gave me. "I'd come to your place but I have to watch at least four more hours of surveillance."

"All right." There's a long pause. "Hey, Milton's having lunch here tomorrow," he says. "Can you come?"

Milton? We've had classes with Milton forever, but we've never hung out with him outside of school. Jealousy surges in my chest. Stupid, I know. "I can't. My grandma will be here all day." *And then there's more exciting film to watch.*

"Oh." He's disappointed, I can tell. So am I. "Okay, well, see ya Monday," he says.

"See ya." I hang up the phone and stare at the frozen black-and-white television screen. Is this what next year will be like if I don't return to Senate? No Jonah, no social life?

Solve the case, soldier, and everything will be fine. As if it's that easy. I toss my drawing pad onto the coffee table and go make popcorn in the microwave, trying to fool my brain into believing that I'm at the movie theater with Jonah and we're watching an action-packed spy thriller. I plop back down on the couch, press Play on the remote, and take a bite of salty, buttery kernels.

But all I taste is stale museum air.

Chapter 14

GLASSES

March 1

I guess the videos aren't a complete waste of time, because yesterday I handed in a picture that got the whole office buzzing. During Saturday's thrilling film festival I saw a man on the Jewish Museum's camera that could have *maybe* been a long-lost cousin of the fluffy-haired guy from the mug shots Bovano showed me. There was something about his nose that seemed familiar, so I decided to draw him just in case.

A lucky guess. Turns out it was the actual perp. Of course Bovano didn't come out and tell me I'd done a good job. I had to find out on my own after a brief insider's moment yesterday at the precinct.

A short blond officer approached me, a friendly grin on his face. He was stout, and resembled a garden gnome. Minus the pointy red hat.

"Eddie, this is unbelievable!" He waved the picture

JACKIE VINCENT

that I drew of the old man. Different hair, reading glasses, a bushy beard. But that nose of his . . . long and crooked, as if broken in several places.

Bovano sprinted out of his office, alarm radiating from his reddening jowls. The gnome saw him and waved.

"Hey, Frank! This kid is amazing! What a picture of Jackie Vincent! Did we know that Jack was hanging around the museums? I thought he had retired . . . Do you think he's still part of the Pic—"

"That's enough, Andy," Bovano snapped, grabbing him by the elbow and shoving him into his office.

After that, Bovano must have held an emergency meeting about me, because now no one will speak to me at the station. They nod or wave politely, but then briskly move away. All conversations cease when I am around. Bovano rules are to be obeyed.

Message clear. I am just a camera. No information whatsoever.

March 2
My mother has lost interest in playing chaperone. She stopped coming to our "sessions" two weeks ago, because it's obvious that 1) I am fine, 2) I haven't been maimed or crippled on the job, 3) I am safe

in the custody of the police, and 4) we are working in art museums, not violent gang areas. If only she could hear Detective Bovano growling at me on the IPODICU.

Today I'm at the Neue Galerie. "All clear," I whisper into my sleeve. I stroll up and down the all-too-familiar rows of glassware and decorative antiques. The place is deserted.

"Copy," Benson replies in my ear bud. He sounds groggy. Maybe he's napping in the van.

I walk back to my easel and draw a little. Today's goblet is slightly more interesting, with crystal leaves curling around the base and up the stem.

Someone in the room sniffs. I turn and see a man with long black hair hunched over one of the display cases, examining antique metal doorknobs. Wait, where did he come from? There are two doors, one on each side of the room, and I thought I was doing a good job monitoring them.

He coughs into a gloved hand. His trench coat collar is turned up, covering the side of his jaw. I can't see his face from where I'm standing.

Long black hair . . . long black hair . . . stringy and pulled back in a sloppy ponytail.

Just like Marco.

My pulse picks up speed. Is it him? The man shifts away from the case and heads for the door. Only one narrow hallway, a twisting staircase, and the main entrance foyer until he reaches the museum exit. He walks by me to leave the room, but the display case between us blocks me from getting any closer. His head is bent down low, fingers pulling his collar up tight around his ears. A very suspicious posture.

I catch a glimpse of the side of his face. The curve of his chin, the length of his nose . . . identical to Marco. No weird beard, but it's him, it has to be. Marco in disguise!

"Detective," I hiss into the microphone on my sleeve. "Detective, I see Marco. Er, the guy with the knife. From the alley." I hate not knowing the names of the suspects. Will Bovano understand what I'm talking about?

Nothing. No response.

I stare down at the blank screen of my IPODICU. Where are the irritated growls? The furrowed eyebrows of death?

I have a bizarre feeling that Bovano is in the bathroom. It's like I've developed a sixth sense about his bodily functions, and that is *NOT* okay.

I am the only line of defense here. The police are counting on me. Time to take action.

"Marco! Marco!" I call as I run after the man. He's up ahead a good thirty feet, moving fast down the fancy stairs toward the large glass exit doors and the free world beyond.

"Marco!"

I don't yell *Stop!* or *Thief!* or *Help!* because my mouth has disconnected from my body and my brain jumped ship back by the glassware.

The suspect is picking up speed. He's landed on the main floor, now just ten feet from the door. He throws a nervous glance over his shoulder. I squint. He's still far away but it's him. And I'm gaining on him.

I start down the stairs, being careful not to trip and fall. "Marco!" I sound like the lunatic kid at the city pool who's playing the Marco Polo game, except no one's yelling *Polo* back and people are just staring. As I reach the landing, a museum guard steps out of the gift shop on my left, watching me with angry eyes. I ignore him and barrel toward the glass exit. Can't he see I'm chasing a thief? And where the heck is Bovano?

Marco is at the door, his gloved hand on the handle. I wish I had something to hurl at him to slow him down. A stick, my canvas, maybe a boomerang. I'm clutching my IPODICU with sweaty fingers and I think about huzzing it at Marco's head, but my aim is terrible and breaking the IPODICU would put me on Bovano's TBK (to be killed) list for sure.

Strong hands grab my shirt and yank me backwards. "What are you doing?" Bovano hisses in an angry whisper.

"The perp, the Marco guy," I say between gasping breaths. I point to the man who is now on the other side of the glass, out on the street, where he'll disappear in a matter of seconds if we don't act now.

"It's not him," Bovano growls.

As if on cue, the man outside turns and looks back at the museum, the winter sky lighting his face. His blue eyes blink at me. Eyes that are not almond shaped. Cheekbones that are not high or pronounced.

He's not Marco. Not even close.

The silence of the Neue Galerie tightens around me like a noose. Could also be the pressure from Bovano's grip, the shaking tension of his fingers sending tremors of *I should strangle you right here and now* down my spine.

He releases me. "You need your eyes checked. And clean your glasses," he snarls as he stomps away, dragging a long piece of toilet paper on his heel. Yep, he was in the bathroom, just like I thought.

The lady from the gift shop is scowling at me over her wire-rimmed reading glasses, and two guards are glaring, arms crossed.

With defeated steps, I climb the stairs back up to the crystal room, back to my stupid sketching charcoal and the stupid goblet.

I don't think we'll be returning to the Neue anytime soon.

Chapter 15

KITTY BARBECUE

March 11

All week I've been paranoid that I'm going to get fired because of the False Alarm Marco Incident. Every time the phone rings at home I think it's Chief Williams calling to kick me off the case. But the chief is as pleasant as ever at the station, and Bovano is business as usual. We even went back to the Neue yesterday and the only thing he muttered was "Don't do anything dumb." It's as if it never happened. He's messing with my mind.

"Ready, Eddie?" Officer Grant says, bringing me out of my thoughts with his usual greeting. He's the older cop who started driving me a few weeks back when my mom stopped chaperoning my museum trips. He's black and thin like me, and looks like he could be my grandfather, so I guess that's why they chose him. We are working undercover, after all.

"Hi, Officer Grant," I say as I settle onto the shiny leather seat of his unmarked police car. I stifle a yawn. Tonight's shift at the Jewish Museum was painfully boring. I think I may have actually fallen asleep while standing up.

Officer Grant shifts the car into gear and slides us into the busy traffic. He's an über-nice guy who lets me ride up front with him right next to the cool knobs and dials, even if I can't touch any of them. And he didn't even yell at me when I got his radio cord all tangled up by accident and set off his siren in the process. He just motioned for me to get in the back. A day later I was riding shotgun again. I'm not sure if he'd forgiven me or just forgotten. He seems pretty old.

I watch the museum fade in the distance behind us. It's getting late, the evening winter sky lit orange from the city lights.

"You catch those bad guys?" he asks with a grin. Another part of our routine. He asks me that question, I smile and shake my head no, and then we drive to my apartment in friendly silence.

Sometimes he stops and buys me candy when he picks up a copy of the *New York Times*. You know things are bad when the only thing you look forward to at the end of a shift is a possible bag of M&M's.

"Just a quick stop," he says as he puts on the blinker and pulls up in front of a convenience store. Looks like tonight is one of those lucky nights.

Opening his car door, he gives me a nod as if to say, *Keep your hands to yourself.* I nod back. I watch as he heads inside the brightly lit store, first pausing to hold a door open for a couple of teenagers. Always kind and polite.

I'm resting in my seat, contemplating new and unusual ways to get even with Robin Christopher, sitting on my hands so I don't touch the shiny buttons on the dash, when a masked man comes running out of the convenience store. Black ski mask, straight from Robbers R Us.

I bolt up, riveted to my view out the windshield. Officer Grant goes running out after him, shouting. The guy heads into an alley (of course!). Officer Grant follows, but slips on some ice, his arms flailing wildly for a brief moment. He loses control, bangs into a trash can, and falls. As I wipe the window that is rapidly fogging up, I can see that he is motionless on the ground.

"Officer down! Officer down!" I scream. No one

hears me. The car is closed up tight. I fumble with the radio to try and call it in, but who am I kidding? I have no idea how this thing works. I start to wildly jab at the buttons, setting off the flashing emergency light (which is on the inside of the car since we're undercover), and blinding myself.

Quickly I try to stuff the red globe under the seat, but the pulsing glow is bouncing off of everything, including my brain, announcing my presence to all criminals within a two-block radius: *Here I am! Worst undercover cop in the world!*

I grope for the door handle and stumble out into the cold night air, banging the door into the truck parked next to us with a loud *thunk*. I hope the owner isn't watching this.

Running toward where he's lying on the pavement, I yell "Officer Grant!" while attempting not to kill myself on the slush and ice. I skid to a panicked halt by the trash can while warily eyeing the dark entrance of the alleyway just a few feet in front of me. I kneel by Officer Grant's body. It appears he has knocked himself out.

I poke him. "Officer Grant?" I think he's breathing. Is that steam coming out of his mouth? Hard to see in the dim light from the store. All of the first aid

I've learned this year is failing me at the moment, so I poke him again.

A clanging noise echoes in the alley, a hollow machine *clank* like a robot zombie is coming. My hand grabs Grant's arm and tugs on him urgently. He's not much help. More rattling. I peer down the dark path; something is definitely there. The robber? A zombie? Or worse? I curse the red strobe light shining behind me from the car, which is clearly calling the attention of whatever evil is stirring in the darkness beyond.

Bang!

Now I'm shaking Grant with both hands, gripping his jacket and yanking him upright and awake for all I'm worth. Which isn't much, because he's not budging.

Do I run? Adult assistance would be good. I'm about to sprint into the store when something black and shiny catches my eye. A Taser attached to Grant's hip. I unsnap it quickly. It's shaped just like a gun so I point the nose into the dark corridor of death and pull the trigger.

Nothing happens.

More banging in the alley. My adrenaline spikes, scouring my brain to get it to figure this out. *Think, Edmund. Think!* There's a switch on the side of the

Taser. A safety. I flip it up and digital numbers come to life by the handle, a red pinprick of light shining out from the front of the barrel. A laser for aiming?

Pointing the weapon into the alley once more, I wrap my finger around the trigger, and squeeze.

Wires on springs shoot out of the gun. The lines must connect with a target, because the whole thing is rigid and pulsating with a current that I can hear.

There's a horrid, ungodly sound of demons being released from hell, a stench of burnt hair, and a flurry of knives that comes at me and slices my arm.

Heroically, I pass out.

"Eddie! Eddie! You all right?" Officer Grant is kneeling over me, his face full of concern.

How long was I out? An hour? Maybe two? My parents must be so worried!

I look at my digital watch. More like eleven seconds.

"That sure was somethin' to see that alley cat take off!" Grant says as he touches the bump on his head and winces. "You went down like a ton of bricks. I was just coming to and was able to grab you. Otherwise you'd have banged yourself up pretty bad."

He stands and helps me up. We're both a little

wobbly. Nothing hurts except my arm. A quick check reveals three slash marks, no doubt inflicted by a fiendish feline.

"We need to get you fixed up," he says, examining the wounds with his reading glasses.

I politely pull away. "It's fine," I say. "My cat Sadie scratches me all the time."

We hobble back to the car like two old men, slip-sliding on the ice and holding each other by the arm. Officer Grant opens the car door for me. The back door of shame. Demoted yet again.

"Sorry, Eddie. I gotta call for backup. An attempted robbery." He points to the mini-mart and then turns off the red light with the flip of a switch. "I'd go and interview the clerk myself, but I can't leave you here alone. Certainly can't drag you in there to talk with witnesses. We'll have to wait until another unit shows."

"I'll tell them I had to use the bathroom," I say, trying to help him out. I have a feeling he'll be in trouble for the chocolate pit stops.

"No need, son," he replies, picking up his radio. "We'll be all right." He calls in the incident. When another police car arrives, he steps out to talk to the cops a moment, then climbs back in. With a loud rev of the engine, he pulls out of the parking lot and turns left instead of right toward my street. My heart lands in my stomach as I realize that he's taking me back to the station. Back to Detective Bovano.

"Can you drop me off first, sir? I'm really tired."

"No chance, Eddie. You were a witness. We won't be long, I promise."

A pang of doom. "We don't need to say anything about the Taser, do we?"

His eyes meet mine in the rearview mirror. "Sorry, kiddo. You discharged my weapon. Not the gun, thank goodness, but we still have to report it. Don't worry . . . it looks a lot worse for me than it does for you. I'm the idiot who knocked myself out."

"Oh," I manage to whisper.

My eyes dart around; my brain whirls to come up with a plan. There's no door handles back here, no escape. No plausible excuse as to why I need to go home *immediately*, if not sooner.

If Jonah Schwartz were in my shoes, he'd jimmy the door open with a pen and jump out of the car at the next traffic light. No exaggeration. By the time we were seven, he could pick the lock on his parents' bedroom door *and* the safe in their office. Amazing what that kid can do with paper clips and some bubble gum.

I go for a different tactic. Much braver and more manly. I bite my fingernails, holding back tears the whole way to the station, knowing one simple truth:

Detective Bovano is going to crucify me.

Chapter 16

BOVANO'S BARBECUE

I can't repeat the exact words that Bovano screams at me, but suffice it to say there are several swears and a whole lot of Italian mixed in.

It's strange, but when he starts to shout I actually feel a little better. It's like the words give me strength. Or maybe I'm just so scared, my mind goes bye-bye.

Regardless, after he gets the yelling out of his system, we come up with four points of agreement from our little "discussion":

1. Eddie Red is never, ever, *ever* again to touch ANY weapon of ANY kind. Ever.

2. Eddie Red's parents do not need to know about this little incident because no harm was done, he meant to help, and his parents might misunderstand and pull him

from the job. (Translation: They are close to cracking the case, and Bovano needs me.)

3. Detective Bovano will now be the one and only driver of Eddie Red.

4. Effective immediately, Eddie Red will begin self-defense lessons as a precautionary measure.

I'm not so thrilled about numbers one and three, but two and four make up for it, so I figure I've come out fifty-fifty.

It's about a hundred degrees in Bovano's office from all the hot angry air. The papers are curling on the bulletin board behind his head. Even his hair has wilted. He mops his brow with his sleeve and takes a slow breath. I think we're finally done hashing this out. Maybe he's out of oxygen. I'm feeling a bit light-headed myself.

"You know," Bovano grunts, leaning back in his chair, shirt buttons straining against what I can only imagine to be a very pale and hairy belly underneath. "I never wanted to take on this mission in the first place. Too much liability. Things get out of hand when a kid is involved. I see that I was correct." He nods his head toward the claw marks on my arm.

I shrug, pulling my shirtsleeve down over the wounds. "It's nothing. Just a scratch. My cat does it all the time."

"Is that what you're gonna say when a bullet grazes you? Or maybe it will be *just a scratch* when a knife punctures an organ? WHAT WERE YOU THINK-ING? YOU COULD HAVE BEEN KILLED!"

Round two, here we go.

He drives me home in silence. When we arrive at my building, I barely manage a "Thanks" before I jump out and scurry over to the protection of my apartment. Eight stairs up to the outer door, a turn of a key, and I'm safe.

Halfway up the staircase, I hear a car door slam. I turn to see that Bovano has left his car in the middle of the street, blue strobe lights on. Abuse of his police privileges, I'd say.

He's coming up the stairs.

I pull out my key but his meaty arm slides past me, a thick finger squashing the buzzer to my apartment.

"Hello?" My mother's voice is tinny over the speaker.

"It's Frank Bovano. I've got Eddie with me."

A weird static scramble resonates over the intercom, as if she's ripping the chain off our apartment door with her teeth. Before you can say Mother Is Panicking, she's standing in front of us. We only live on the second floor, but seriously. It's like she strapped on a jetpack.

"Frank?" she says, in a tone that's a combination of *What have you done now, Edmund?* and *Oh my God, my son has been murdered* even though I'm standing right in front of her. My dad joins her in the doorway, no doubt concerned after she clawed the door open and flew down the stairway. I don't know what her problem is. I'm only about thirty minutes later than usual. Is it because Bovano is here?

"Evening, Joyce, Herb," Bovano says as I try to squeeze through the entrance and flee the scene. The hulking mass that is my father blocks me. His mustache twitches the way it does when he knows I am up to something.

I realize that I am not playing it cool like we discussed at the station. I sense Bovano's dark eyes burning into my back. He clears his throat. I turn back to peek at him, positioning my body as close to my father as humanly possible.

"Sorry he's a bit late," Bovano says, hat in hand. "We had to talk about the case. That's why I drove him tonight. Eddie's been a big help, and I find it's good to bounce some ideas off him, so I'll be driving him home from now on."

"Oh," my mom says brightly, beaming down at me as if I just won the Nobel Prize. Then she smiles at Bovano and says, "Frank, would you like to come in for coffee and pie?"

I just about die on the spot. Detective Bovano having a snack in my kitchen is beyond my wildest nightmares. *Great, Mom. Let's have him over for movies and popcorn. Maybe he can snuggle up on the couch, too. Don't be surprised when I end up in therapy, crazy lady.*

"Thanks, but I'll have to pass. Busy day tomorrow. Oh, and one more thing. We're trying out a new 'Safety for Kids' program, teaching them about self-defense. We were hoping that Eddie here could be our test model. Help us fine-tune the program. Plus they're great skills to have for any kid living in the city."

He's good. A little *too* good.

My parents are ecstatic and start to blather on about how wonderful it will be for my self-esteem.

They don't know it's so I can fight off alley cats because I am the lamest undercover cop ever.

Detective Bovano says good night: a handshake for my dad, a mushy smile for my mom, a grizzled look of death for me, and he's gone.

I shoot my mom a glare and sprint for the apartment. My arm is on fire.

Four Band-Aids and a whole lot of disinfectant later, I head for the kitchen. Crime-fighting works up quite an appetite. I just pray I don't get some kind of weird alley cat infection. Maybe I'll ask about the signs of rabies in science class tomorrow.

I load my plate with a turkey sandwich, grapes, yogurt, and two brownies, then join my parents on the sofa. They're cuddling and watching a police detective movie (not my favorite type at the moment), oblivious to the evening I've just had. Mom doesn't even comment that I'm eating on the couch or having double dessert. When I'm done, they kiss me and send me to bed, business as usual. No suspicion whatsoever.

Sadie knows.

Instead of hissing her usual greeting as I approach the stairs to my room, she freezes, the hair rising on her back. Maybe she smells singed fur on my clothing. She moves away from me slowly, never taking her eyes off me, and then zooms down the hallway, her marshmallow fluff tail tucked between her legs. A small victory in an otherwise awful day.

I never do see Officer Grant again, which is too bad because I enjoyed his company. I hear he's taking an early retirement this May.

Chapter 17

PIZZA

———

March 18

"Edmund, it's time to stir things up," Jonah announces to me on our bus ride home from school. We both take the city bus over to the Upper West Side.

"They need you. It's obvious. They're getting closer to cracking the case. Otherwise they'd have fired you by now. Especially after the Taser." *Tap-tap-tappity-tap.* He's tapping a pen on the window. The lady in front of us shoots him a dirty look.

I can't focus on police work right now. Not because it's über-boring, which it is (alley cats and Marco chases aside), but because we've started a unit on hands in art class, and my universe is imploding.

Jenny Miller is my "hands partner."

All during art class I was on the verge of throwing up from nerves, and I don't know how I'm going to do this for the next few weeks. Of course I can't tell Jonah about it because he would be unbelievably embarrassing about the whole thing. So I suffer in silence, my hands a sweaty mess. Even now just thinking about it.

The hand is one of the most difficult things to draw. There are so many lines and textures and veins that no matter how you do it, it rarely looks lifelike. It just flops down on the page, flat and fake.

We took turns today. I had to study and draw Jenny's hands, and then she did the same for me. In both scenarios, my stomach was ready to exit through my mouth, and I could barely breathe.

I have my mother's hands. Thin and delicate, no strength whatsoever. You can imagine how psyched I am about *that*. My parents tell me that I have artist's hands, and that if they were big and awkward then I couldn't draw well.

It's not very reassuring.

At one point Jenny shifted my hand, actually making contact with it. She might as well have used a cattle prod, because I jumped about ten feet. I have to relax or she's going to think I'm a major head case.

"Earth to Edmund!" Jonah says while tappity-tapping on my baseball cap with his pen.

"Quit it, Jonah!" I smack his hand away.

"We need to break in to Bovano's office." His leg jiggles up and down, banging my knee and sending tremors of hectic Morse code down into my shoes. "And I have a plan."

"I'll do it myself," I say quickly. "I know Bovano's routine. After I give him my reports he always leaves to make photocopies and—"

"We buy some pizza," he continues as if I haven't spoken. "I go in dressed as a delivery boy, luring all the cops, including Bovano, away from their work with the promise of stuffed crust goodness. You zip into the office and steal the info off the board. A smash-and-grab job with a pizza decoy. How much money do you have in the bank? The whole operation will cost about a hundred bucks. No problem. I have twenty in my sock drawer. I can ask my dad for at least twenty more. Now draw me a picture of the station and Bovano's office so I know how to get around."

I ignore the request. "Give me a week," I say. Jonah showing up in that office would be a major disaster. But I do agree it's time to take action and search for more information. I'm only up to a measly $703.25 in earnings (an über-awesome amount of money on a normal day, but Senate costs *waaaay* more) and the first tuition payment is due next month. My parents said they could cover it for now, but time is running out.

"My stop is next!" Jonah says, throwing on his backpack and nearly clipping my ear. "Promise you'll make something happen. Be all you can be, soldier! Promise, or else I'm ordering the pizza uniform on eBay. I found a good one. Operation Pepperoni is on the horizon!"

I sigh. "Fine."

I pity George Gyukeri, who is Jonah's hands partner, because Jonah literally can't stop moving, especially his hands. All through class I heard George yapping at him to stay still, which actually helped with my Jenny-nerves.

As the bus pulls away, I watch Jonah on the street. He reminds me of a dancing leprechaun with that red hair of his, jumping over lines, trying to make it home without stepping on any fateful cracks. He gives me a huge wave seconds before he collides with an old man, sending them both tumbling into a street lamp. Jonah turns neon red and wraps his arms around the man's torso as if to steady him, but he's just knocking him more off-balance. The poor guy must feel like he's being groped by a hyper chimpanzee.

The man seems fine. He holds on to the post and waves Jonah away, probably to prevent further harm. I start to laugh in wheezing gasps. It feels like I haven't laughed with Jonah in forever. We need to hang out this weekend, have a sleepover and forget all about police business. A chance to be regular kids and build couch cushion forts, or dare each other to drink orange juice mixed with milk.

As my laughter turns into snorting chuckles, the same disapproving woman on the bus raises a shame-on-you eyebrow at me.

I snap my mouth closed, my cheeks hot with embarrassment. I wasn't laughing at a senior citizen in dire straits; I was laughing at Jonah's ridiculous spaziness. Is that bad karma?

I sure hope not, because between the Taser incident and Jonah's pizza plan, I need all the good karma I can get.

Chapter 18

SPY

———

March 23

My mom is dragging me to an art opening tonight, which I am not thrilled about. I spend way too much time in museums these days. It's actually becoming unhealthy. I need some sun, or I'm going to come down with scurvy or leprosy or whatever disease you catch when you need more vitamins.

Mom's not buying my excuse. Her office is sponsoring a photography show at the Winston Café, and it is crucial that I be there, or else clients may abandon the company and the earth might stop spinning. I can't complain, though, since she did let me become Eddie Red and I guess I owe her big-time.

At the exhibit, I weave my way through the city coats, designer purses, and tacky comments like "What an inspired angle!" so I can check out what everyone is raving about. The *artist* (and I use the term lightly here) has taken black-and-white photos of body parts, blown them up so you barely know what they are, and then scattered the shots along two walls. It looks like a giant was sucked into a lawn mower, chopped into pieces, and then spit out into a tunnel for all to admire.

"Have you ever seen such artistic vision?" a too-thin woman gushes.

It's an arm, lady. And an ugly one at that.

My mom gives me an enthusiastic wave from across the room. She's stunning in a red wool suit and knee-high black boots. One of the guys from her office clearly thinks so too, the way he keeps offering her a drink. My dad swoops in to rescue her, directing her to the dance floor.

I wave to her and head for the food table. They always serve super-tiny food at these things, as if dinner in miniature is supposed to taste better. A feast fit for Stuart Little.

I pick up a mini pie that has melted cheese on it. Looks promising. After popping it in my mouth, I nearly gag. Über-gross. Pretty sure it's stuffed with cat food. As I discreetly spit it into a napkin, a woman with green eyes catches me in the act and grins. I duck my head in embarrassment and toss my napkin into a garbage can, then beeline for the table of sodas. My mom can't complain this time. I need calories.

It's a little bizarre how the lady continues to watch me, like she really *knows* me. She seems familiar too, but I can't place her. Her emerald gaze is freaking me out.

When I get back home, I draw her.

I inspect the picture for an hour, poring over every inch of it, willing myself to find her in a scene from my mind. Nothing fits. It's like flipping through a database at high speed and then the computer crashes. My brain is fried. Those green eyes are unforgettable, and yet I'm forgetting. I wonder: Is it possible to get Alzheimer's at age eleven?

I have to remember that I am an undercover spy. A lame one, to be sure, but being a spy involves a whole new world of awareness. People may recognize me and I may be in danger. I need to prepare myself.

March 24

Armed with this new paranoia and the pizza peer pressure from Jonah, I go to Bovano's office the next day. *Don't take no for an answer. You are Eddie Red. Don't take no for an answer.*

"I need more information," I announce, handing him my report.

The typical sneer starts to curl the corner of his

GREEN-EYED LADY

mouth. "Tell me you're talking about the Yankees' preseason schedule, kid. Tell me you're not asking about the investigation. I cannot and *will not* give you more information about the case. You are a camera only. You're in and you're out. Now, out!" He stabs a finger through the air, motioning to the door.

I am not going quietly. "Detective Bovano, I have all these pictures in my head, and it would be so much better if I knew why we were looking for these guys. Are there crime scenes from the past I could analyze? Maybe I could study some clues to see where they'll strike next. There's this woman I saw last night, and I swear I know her from the case, but I just can't piece it together. If only—"

"No, Eddie. That's *my* job. To piece it together. We're done here." He opens the office door and gestures with his head.

Plan B.

I walk out of his office and over to the water cooler on the far side of the room, pretending to get a drink until Bovano lumbers out of his cave a minute later. He always goes to the fourth floor to make copies of my pictures, so I know I have a few minutes.

"Marilyn, I forgot my jacket. Do you mind?" I ask

his secretary, who smiles and waves me back into the office, her head buried in paperwork.

My heart is hammering in my ears. *Act casual!*

I go up to the papers on the wall and start to take mental pictures. A map with thumbtacks in it. *Click.* Museum Mile. *Click.*

I peer out at Marilyn, who is busy typing. I open the files on Bovano's desk. *The Picasso Gang. Click.* More pictures of the blond guy from the mug shots. *Click.* A book on geometry. A book on ancient Egypt. Huh?

Click-click-click.

I am there for thirty seconds, my pulse racing the entire time. "Thanks!" I practically shout at Marilyn as I flee my crime scene. She gives another wave, not noticing my jittery behavior.

It's not until I'm out on the street that I relax.

You did it, Eddie Red. You did it! He didn't catch you. You're not such a loser spy after all. Now go home and start writing it all down.

Unforeseen Problem #1: None of it makes any sense.

Chapter 19

KUNG FU ROCKS

Unforeseen Problem #2: My grades are starting to slip.

March 25

I completely spaced my science lab report, and Mr. Pee won't give me an extension. He may still be bitter about the cafeteria puddle incident.

I failed a spelling quiz in English, which is pathetic, because one glance at the list of words and I've got it. I just forgot to look at the stupid list. And then I used the word *über* in math class and Mrs. Reed got mad and threatened my participation grade. Report cards come out in three weeks, and I have to seriously get it together or my mom will yank me from the police force.

Art class is no longer my place of peace, mostly because I'm fighting a losing battle with the barf-knots in my gut.

Jenny studies my hands for a while, this time in a position like I'm holding a pen. We're learning about Escher's *Hands* piece today, the one of the hands drawing each other. I watch as her blue eyes dart from my hands to the page, her brow wrinkled in concentration. I can count her freckles from where I'm sitting. Not that I would do that. When did I become such a lovesick idiot?

She chews her pencil pensively, her lips a candy shade of pink. I wonder if Happy Kat Cat pencils contain lead or other toxins. I hope not. But it seems like something an evil cat company might put together.

Suddenly she speaks and I almost slide off of my chair. "I have something for you, Edmund," she says, smiling and reaching into her bag.

She hands me a Happy Kat Cat eraser.

"I notice you use an eraser a lot. I thought you'd like a new one."

"Thanks," I say. Jenny Miller has given me a present. It's a cat, but nobody's perfect. She's given me a present!

I sit there and look at it, trying to think of something intelligent to say. The more the clock ticks on, the more I just appear to be a moron who is staring at an eraser.

"Edmund hates cats," blurts a voice from behind my shoulder. "Don't you know that? Everybody knows that!"

Jenny blushes and apologizes before I can turn around and knock the voice's block off.

Thank you, Jonah Schwartz.

Spanish class isn't much better. We're studying adjectives: singulars, plurals, masculine, feminine, colors, you know the drill. We have to go around the room and say things about different people, like *Jonah es heróico*. (His sentence, not mine.)

If I hear *"Edmundo es bajo"* one more time, I may lose it. (*Bajo* means "short," in case you didn't know.) Pick another adjective. How about *guapo*? *Inteligente*? Heck, I'd even take the occasional *estúpido*. There are other words out there, people.

Eric Johnson is just as short as I am but he's built like the son of Zeus and is awesome at every sport on the planet, so the teacher says *"Eric es atletico"* and the girls make swooning noises. And I'm stuck with *"Edmundo es bajo"* and no one sighs with admiration.

But the promise of kung fu wisdom is giving me strength.

Okay, it's not truly kung fu. It's just self-defense moves, but close enough.

After school my mom takes me to the station. She decided to tag along for my first self-defense lesson because she heard the words "sparring mat" and translated that to mean "Edmund is playing with knives and *WILL* die," so she's here to observe.

I change into sweats in the bathroom, then head to the police training gym, psyched to get cracking and work out some aggression from the Kat eraser disaster. I debate whether to tie a cool Karate Kid bandanna around my head. Maybe not. Might come off as a bit desperate.

My mom lifts an eyebrow at the shiny weaponry hanging on the walls but says nothing, taking a seat on a red bench by the boxing gloves.

I walk into the middle of the blue floor mat and start to stretch. It seems like the appropriate thing to do. I breathe deeply and close my eyes, awaiting my Master, my Sensei, my Guru of All Things Ninja.

In walks Detective Bovano.

I guess I must look stunned to see him (which I am), because he starts to guffaw right then and there, slapping his knee and laughing his head off.

"You were expecting Mr. Miyagi?" he snorts, his big belly bouncing up and down at his joke.

I stare at him blankly, then avert my eyes. Detective Bovano is a scary man on any day, but seeing him in a police-issue gym suit is über-alarming. The cotton-polyester blend is not very forgiving around his waistline, and we'll just leave it at that.

My mom is giggling as well, as if some sort of dumb grownup joke has transpired about me that I don't get, and I am annoyed. I step up in front of him and square my shoulders.

He stops laughing. "You think you're gonna fight me, eh? All right, Eddie, let's see what you've got."

What? What *I've* got? I've got nothing. That's why I'm here. To get something.

I shrug and get into my best defensive stance, knees bent, fists up. What now?

He pulls up his droopy pants and leans in, hands on his thighs so he can look me in the eye. "Eddie," he whispers, "there is only one move that we are going to learn here today. I am going to tell you about this one move, and every time you get into a sticky situation, it will save you. It's called the Nike defense. Are you ready?"

Nike defense? Sounds athletic and über-cool. I nod eagerly. I am ready.

I tilt toward him, hanging on to his every word. Unfortunately his wisdom is laced with breath that smells like salami and garlic.

"Run away, Eddie."

I straighten up. "What?"

"I want you to run away. As a child, you cannot possibly defend yourself. The movies have lied to you, Eddie. You think a kick to the privates, or an elbow to the nose is going to help you? You'll miss, and the perp will be ready and hopped up on adrenaline and God knows what else. They will knock you down. And then you'll be . . ." He pauses for dramatic effect:

"In trouble."

"Detective, I thought you were going to teach me some moves," I protest. I glance over at my mom, like maybe she'll confirm this statement. She's busy texting, lost in a world of real estate transactions. Suddenly her phone rings. She stands and walks to the other side of the gym, chatting merrily about a brownstone on the Upper East Side, abandoning me to my doom.

"I'm going to teach you to run. I know kids, and I know they want to fight. At least, they *think* they want to fight. Just like in the movies. But you need to learn to run before someone levels you and you can't. You want to be a hero, Eddie, I can see that. You tried to be one when you grabbed that Taser like a tough guy. So that's why we're here. To teach you to do the right thing. And run."

My jaw clenches; I want blood. This is the most bogus self-defense lesson I've ever heard of.

Bovano squats lightly on the balls of his feet. "All right, I'm going to try to rob you. You see me coming. Do you run, or throw an elbow?" He lunges at me, all three hundred pounds of Italian meatball. I try to block him and bring my elbow to his face. He sweeps his leg under mine and flattens me on my stomach.

"If you had run, you'd be safe," he hisses in my ear. My body convulses on the mat. I scramble to my feet, spinning to face him again.

"Now I'm a creep in a parking lot, following you,"

he says. "Do you run, or try a karate kick like you've seen in the movies?" He slinks around the mat edge, pretending to be a stalker.

Slowing my breathing through my nose, I summon the spirits of karate. I lift my leg up like a ninja crane, ready to strike. Anger races through my veins. I want to kick his teeth in.

Bovano grabs my kicking leg and flips me onto my back. The slam of my spine on the mat knocks the wind out of my lungs. He squats next to me as I lie there paralyzed and dying.

"If you had run, you'd be safe. Now you're roadkill. Get up!" he barks.

I get to my knees, coughing, eyes watering in the direction of my mom. She's still a good twenty feet away, frowning off into space with the phone pressed by her ear. Where's the motherly panic? The protection? I'm getting my butt handed to me by a grownup here—an officer of the law, of all people! She and I are going to have serious words tonight.

"Do you get it now, Eddie? *You run*. You always run. Until you are all grown up. And judging by your size . . ." He scrutinizes me and smirks. "You should probably run when you're an adult as well." He chuckles.

I am seriously going to kill this man.

I crouch, teeth bared, legs bent, like a tiger ready to pounce, my body tense with rage. *Use what you have, Edmund. A low center of gravity. Lure him in, knock him off-balance.*

Bovano sees me ready myself, his exasperation showing in his red blotchy skin and darkening expression. He's had enough of our lesson. Eyes bulging, he comes at me like he's got a knife in his hand.

Kick him! my brain screams.

I focus all energy, all of my puny wimp power, and kick hard as he lunges. He trips on the edge of the mat and my foot makes contact with his groin. With a yelp, he crumples to the floor.

"Oops," I say, instantly regretting this entire situation.

My mom rushes over. "Frank . . . Frank, are you okay?"

Sure, *now* she clues in to what's happening.

She kneels by his trembling body, giving him a few friendly pats on the back. I shuffle over to stand safely behind her, anxiety squeezing my lungs (which are still not working at full capacity, by the way).

This was not what I intended. I just wanted a karate lesson, for Pete's sake.

"Hmph," Bovano huffs, pulling himself into the fetal position, eyes still closed. He lies there, breathing hard.

My mom bites her lip. It's obvious she doesn't know what to do. Girls just don't understand these things.

Ice? Heat? Either way, I'm not offering to help hold it in place.

"It's probably better to let him be, let him breathe," she whispers to me.

Sounds like a good idea. Learn to run? I am running outta here, and never coming back. Once he gains his composure, I am a dead man.

She turns to Bovano and leans over his body. "Frank, I think we'll go now, and leave you to your . . . self."

She throws me a stern look, gesturing with her head. My cue:

"Sorry, Detective Bovano," I whimper.

Thus endeth the lesson.

Chapter 20

SUNDAY STUDIES

March 27

You can probably hear Jonah's laughter across Central Park. I'm glad _he_ thinks it's funny.

I, however, am completely traumatized, having slept only five hours the past two nights. I'm not sure if I can face Bovano again, but I have to because the picture of the lady with the green eyes is haunting me. Bovano holds the key, I'm sure of it.

A knock sounds on the door. "Boys, I hope you're not playing video games," my mom's voice calls.

"No, Mom. We're playing Demons and Warlocks."

"Okay, then. Let me know if you want a snack. I'll be in the kitchen." I hear her retreat down the hallway.

It works every time, like a parent-repellant spray. She knows better than to interrupt a card game of

Demons and Warlocks. Jonah will assault her with random factoids about the talking tree that shoots fireballs that he invented, or insist on showing her the cool Snake-Demon card that he bought the other day. She'll have to stand there politely nodding for an hour.

I'm glad she left, because there is no covering up the evidence in here. One peek and she'd know we are most definitely *not* playing Demons and Warlocks. I would call this game Skinny Kids and Bad Guys. There's a mountain of papers spread out on my bed, along with a bright smear of mug shots and color-coded flash cards plastered on my wall. Jonah finally slept over last night, and after breakfast this morning we came into my room and have been sitting here for four hours, which is astounding for someone with his attention span.

Everything I've drawn from my office espionage is laid out. Jonah has organized it into neat piles and then written down categories and subcategories and pinned them up so he can do further analysis. The kid is in heaven.

I have every picture I've sketched for the police (I made copies on my mother's scanner). Some are mug shots of the known criminals, some are random (like that guy who stole the canvas from me—I saw his face later on the surveillance tape) and some are my own personal suspects, like the green-eyed woman from the photography exhibit. There's something about her that's creeping me out. Call it a hunch.

Turns out the four suspects Bovano showed me in the beginning are a group of thieves known as the Picasso Gang. I saw that name along with their pictures in a folder on his desk. I write down what I know about them:

The Picasso Gang
1. Asian guy— "Marco"
2. Older, crazy-haired guy—Jackie Vincent
3. Bald guy—knife perp from alley with Dad
4. Blond guy—Heinrich. The leader?

I frown at my notes. Somehow listing everyone as "guy" seems like pathetic police work, but I still don't have many names. I managed to see the last name *Heinrich* on Bovano's desk, written on a file that contained pictures of the blond man, black-and-white shots of him out to lunch at an outdoor café of some kind. In Europe? He looks European with his short-trimmed beard and black turtleneck.

"What do the dots even mean?" Jonah wonders aloud, gesturing to a map of Museum Mile that we pinched from my parents' New York City survival stash. I drew circles in pencil on two museums, sites that Bovano had marked with a thumbtack on the original. The Neue Galerie and the Jewish Museum. My two least favorite places in the world at the moment. Plus more circles on cafés across the street from those sites. Seven spots total.

"And why are the cafés marked?" he continues. "Are they places that have been robbed? Or places where this gang has been seen, wandering around? We need to figure this out."

"Wait—" I start to say as he traces my circles with black permanent marker. I end my protest with a sigh. I guess we won't be returning the map.

We keep looking for patterns, but it all seems random. Just two parallel lines running down Fifth Avenue and Madison.

The block where the ice cream incident took place is not marked. That was over on Lexington Ave., three

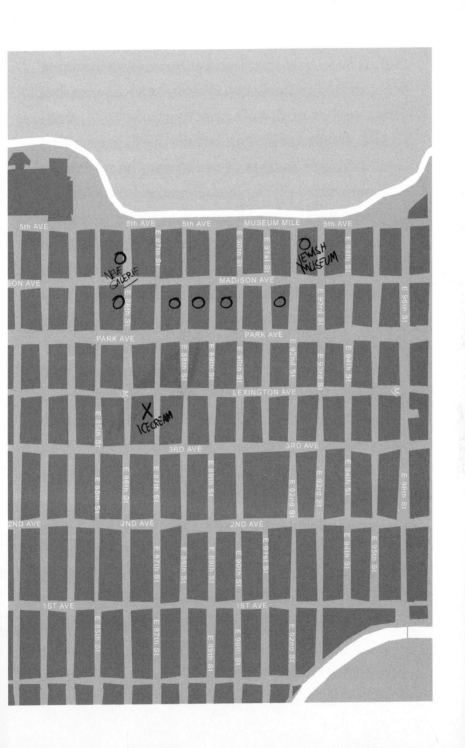

streets away from the museums. Obviously the police don't think it's important. Jonah decides to mark it with a big black X, for a caution marker.

The geometry book on Bovano's desk is a mystery, as is the Egyptian book. Jonah's theory is that Bovano is looking for a pattern on the map, some sort of geometrical shape that will tip him off as to where the next robbery will take place. The sites along Museum Mile form a long tube. I tell him it could be an obelisk, which would explain the Egyptian book. But the top point of the obelisk would land in the middle Madison Avenue, so that doesn't fit.

We come up with a list of research that will be done over the next week. My dad is, after all, a librarian, and I'm sure we can use the database at the library he used to work at. They're still on good terms.

I write down the major questions:

1. Have there been robberies at these locations?

2. Do the circles form a pattern that predicts where the ultimate heist will take place?

3. Is the green-eyed lady important, or am I losing my mind?

If we can't come up with any answers, I'll have to go back to Bovano's office and sneak around again. Or Jonah will attempt his pizza plan, which makes me break out in a cold sweat whenever I think about it.

"Son, I'm very proud of you. I don't think I tell you that enough."

"Thanks, Dad."

We're at the library later that afternoon and he's getting all emotional on me. I can tell that he's psyched I've asked for his help. Usually I reject his library geek-outs completely.

I wonder if he'd be so proud of me if he knew that I stole information from Bovano, Tasered a cat, and am currently lying through my teeth to him.

I have him working on the geometrical shape problem. I told him it was for math class, to figure out what two parallel lines can form as a shape, given other lines that intersect with them. Meanwhile I'm scouring the newspaper database for recent New York

City robberies. We're side by side, typing in computer cubbies with a partition between us, but we might as well be working at the same desk, because he keeps leaning over into my personal space to "share" his discoveries. It's worse than sitting next to Jonah.

"You know, Edmund, not all geometrical shapes are based on their perimeters," he says as he swivels his chair into my cubby. "Are you sure these lines intersect with others? Do they have closed sides like a rectangle? Some shapes are open ended. Like a balbis."

"A what?"

"A balbis. A shape like an H . . . two parallel lines connected by a third. Like rugby posts. Know what I mean?"

"Yep. Not the shape I'm searching for, though." *Come on, Dad! Stay focused!* I knew this mission would be risky. The man can seriously mentally derail and tool away on random stuff for hours.

He scratches his mustache. "There's also shapes within shapes. Triangles that have circles inscribed in them, called the incircles of the triangle. Are you sure it's just two parallel lines? Could be triangles within a rectangle. Circles within that."

I'm not sure about any of it. Shapes within shapes? This is insane. I'm hoping Jonah has more luck.

"What are you working on?" My father peers over my shoulder.

"I'm researching crime in New York City for history class. Art museum robberies. Mr. Daniels asked us to research New York history, and I guess I got interested because of my job."

He buys the lie and returns to his computer to help me look up stuff about Museum Mile.

Lying is second nature to me these days, which I'm not too happy about. I hope in the end there's some sort of good karma that comes from solving the case, or I have some serious repentance to do with the Big Man Upstairs.

Dad's phone rings. Not so much rings as plays a jazzy tune that mortifies me every time it happens.

"Hi, honey. What's that? All right, I'll tell him. Yep, we'll be home right away."

He grins at me over the partition as he ends the call. "Good news, Edmund. The police are taking you out to dinner tonight. A thank-you present for all of your hard work. We're all invited. Let's go home and get changed."

I force a smile. I'm sure this has something to do with Detective Bovano and my ill-fated kick during self-defense class. Having dinner with that man is the last thing I want to do. And doesn't a thank-you dinner happen at the end, when you've solved the case and everyone wants to celebrate?

I don't know what to make of this invitation, but I don't like it. I'm going to make my father taste all of my food before I eat it. Who knows what Bovano is capable of.

Chapter 21

GELATO

———

Of course we meet Bovano at an Italian restaurant and *of course* he sits across from my mother. My dad sits next to her, a friendly smile on his face. How is he so oblivious to this creepy date scenario that Bovano is working here?

That leaves one seat left for me, next to Bovano at our cozy table for four.

Hooray.

After some small talk and pleasantries, my parents lean their heads together and start to whisper about what they want to order. They do this annoying thing about ordering to share, as if neither of them can actually just have their own food.

I sit and fiddle with my watch. Should I say something about the kick? Did he hear my apology at the gym, or was he in a pain-induced blackout? Should I apologize again?

Bovano beats me to it. "Do you remember what you learned from our self-defense class?"

I nod.

"Good. Always run, Eddie. Always run. If you understand that, then there will be no more need for those classes."

I nod again, although I'm not happy about it. I still want to learn some good old- fashioned butt-kicking techniques. And I do regret hurting him. "Detective, I—"

He holds his hand up as if to say *Fuggeddaboutit. We never speak of it again.*

Fine by me. I'll go take classes at the Y.

There is little pleasure in eating my ravioli. Bovano is left handed, so we keep bumping elbows, which results in a frown cast in my direction followed by a bout of cramps in my stomach.

Bump—glare— "Sorry"—cramp—cramp.

Partway through dessert, I start to sweat. From the rich food? I've barely eaten. And the restaurant isn't hot, either, even with the cheesy fake fire blowing in the middle of the dining room, or the pizza door opening and closing. Did Bovano poison me as I feared? I haven't taken my eyes off my food, and he hasn't taken his eyes off my mother, so I don't think he could have managed it.

It's like I'm in a dream. I observe the grownups' faces at the table, detaching myself from the scene, becoming a fly on the wall. Or a fly in hot olive oil — choose your metaphor. Dad is spewing out random factoids about Sicily to Bovano, whose parents were born there. Huh, he actually has parents. And here I thought he'd just sprung up from the earth in an angry ball of flame.

Bovano is nodding his head, casting flirtatious looks at my mom and interjecting an opinion when he can, while my mom smiles back, her dimples lighting up Bovano's world.

Things have ground to a strange slow motion, my brain desperate to make sense of the alarm in my gut: the clink of the silverware, my father's chuckle, the flicker of candlelight, a drop of sweat running down my temple. Something is coming. Something is not right.

"I'm afraid I come bearing bad news, folks." Bovano's voice snaps me back to reality. "This case we've been working on . . . No harm in telling you a bit about it. We've been tracking a group of art thieves, all led by a German pro named Lars. An international thief, famous for playing with the cops, setting them up with clues to make the crime coincide with a geometric pattern on a map. Drove the French crazy a while back."

My dad glances at me and quirks his mustache at the word "geometric," but says nothing.

Bovano continues. "Eddie has helped, he really has . . ."

Warning bells sound in my head. There's a big "but" coming my way.

"I wanted to let you know what we're up against," he says, "and how grateful we are for your help. But the case is going to be dropped soon. And so will Eddie's contract. No results means no money. The department can't afford more time. We officially close up shop mid-May. If we don't solve this thing in the next seven weeks, then it's all over."

Senate Academy . . . classes and lunches and bus rides with Jonah . . . gone. My throat tightens. *Do not get upset, Edmund!* I command myself.

My parents murmur words of understanding, as if everything is going to be fine. No harm done. But they're not the ones whose world has just been shattered. I should get a T-shirt: I WORKED FOR THE NYPD AND ALL I GOT WAS A LOUSY ITALIAN DINNER AND SOME VERBAL ABUSE.

I study Bovano, wondering whether he has invented this challenge as some kind of test to push me. His face is blank. He asks for the check and makes up an excuse about having to get back to the office.

He leaves without looking at me.

We stand to go, my mom wrapping her arm around my waist. "We're so proud of you, honey," she says. "You're such a hard worker. Don't worry, there's still time."

Still time? Yeah, right. I've been at this for months with zero progress.

"Maybe you and I can go out for ice cream next week. It's been a while," my dad says, patting my back. "I wonder if they received a new shipment of pistachio."

Pistachio!

Suddenly it all clicks together. *That's* where I know the green-eyed woman from. From the alley crime I witnessed, the ice cream date with my dad. She was there! She walked right by the bench just before the men fought in the alley. Is she connected to the Picasso Gang? If she is, she might have been casing the Winston Café at my mom's art show, although I don't think any of those photographs were worth stealing.

My spirits lift as we walk to the subway. This isn't over. I still have seven weeks. I figured out the green-eyed lady connection that's been hounding me, which is a huge relief. Now I have to uncover if she fits into the gang. And more important, tonight Bovano made a mistake. He used the name *Lars*. I know the last name Heinrich from the pictures on Bovano's desk. New clues, new information. I can do this!

There's an extra bounce in my step as we head home. My parents smile at each other, happy to think that they raised such a well-adjusted kid who doesn't get upset when things don't go his way.

Little do they know what I'm plotting.

Chapter 22

OFFICE WORK

After I change into pajamas and say good night to my parents, I settle into my desk chair and fire up the computer. The search for "Heinrich" that resulted in a dead end last week is now exploding with possibilities when I type in "Lars Heinrich."

Turns out Lars has been a very busy man, or at least he was thirty years ago. I examine his face, research his crimes. He's the blond guy in the mug shot, all right, but he hasn't been seen since the eighties.

Maybe he's had drastic plastic surgery. I should do some drawings of what he might look like if he had a chin lift, a nose job, cheek and forehead implants . . . What other crazy things do people have done to their faces?

He's a suspect for robberies in Rome, Paris, and Amsterdam, but the cops could never get enough evidence to charge him, let alone convict him of the

LARS MUGSHOT

heists. Diamonds, artwork . . . an ancient Roman statue. Who is this guy? How can you steal a six-foot stone statue and not get caught?

Thinking of Bovano's book on ancient Egypt, I scroll to find a link connecting Lars with Cairo or a pharaoh's tomb or the Nile River. Nothing.

I study intricate European maps, the city streets where he planned his crimes. I am a Googling ninja until well after midnight. Just when I think I can't possibly read another page from a French newspaper (of which I understand *non*), a list of Parisian museums and restaurants that were robbed in the eighties slaps me across the face. The word "Picasso" is repeated over and over again, listing the artwork that was stolen from each location. I guess that's why they're called the Picasso Gang. The robbery sites are laid out on a city map of Paris, forming a star surrounded by a circle, a perfect geometric figure.

I recognize the shape from a tattooed kid who rides the bus uptown. He's got piercings and tons of body ink, radiating an aura of I-will-kill-you-if-you-look-at-me. The star and circle pattern is tattooed on his forearm. Maybe Lars was a troubled youth back in the day?

I look it up online. A pentagram, or five-sided star, used for religious and cult purposes. If the two points of the star are facing upward, it's connected with devil worship. I toggle back to the map of Paris. The two points are facing up.

I am out of my league.

March 28

I wake up wired. The pressure is on, and it's making me more daring and bolder. Reckless, even. *Nobody* is going to keep me from Senate and Jonah and whatever awesome things we'll do next year. I may not be able to outwit Lars Heinrich, or Satan for that matter, but I *will* get Frank Bovano to hear what I have to say.

Operation Green Eyes kicks off after school at the police station.

"I need to see the detective!" I yell in Marilyn's direction as I fly by her desk and into Bovano's office.

"Eddie, he's on the phone! You don't have an appoint—"

I close the door swiftly behind me.

Bovano is at his desk, phone by his ear, mouth open in shocked irritation. I just stand there in the middle of the office, ignoring my brain as it yells,

What are you doing? Run, you idiot! He will eat you alive!

"Jim, I'll have to call you back." He hangs up, shooting fireballs out his eyes at me. "Getting a little comfortable in my office, are we, Eddie?"

"Sir, I'm sorry. But I have new information about the case. A green-eyed woman walked by me in January when I was eating ice cream with my dad, right before those guys in the alley started to yell. And then I saw her at the Winston Café last week. At a photography exhibit. Look!"

I place the picture I drew of her onto his desk, then retreat to the center of the room again, making sure to keep a safe distance between us. "She's mixed up in this, I know it. She's part of the—" I almost say *Picasso Gang* and blow the whole thing.

He frowns at the picture, then shoves it back at me with a scowl. "She's not a suspect."

"But she could be! I've seen her twice now. At an art show and a crime scene. She's involved!"

"She's not involved. Look, I don't know what angle you're working here, but I have a job to do. Go home."

Angle . . . angle . . . The word tickles at a memory. I shake my head. *Stay focused!*

"No," I say boldly. I fold my arms and stand my ground. The door is only three feet behind me in case I need to run.

"*What?*"

"No, sir. I am onto something."

"Eddie, in case you didn't hear me last night, we are down to the wire here. If we don't get a break in the case, they are closing us down. I do *not* have time to chase down your little theories. YOU ARE NOT A DETECTIVE."

"Maybe I should ask Chief Williams about it. See if *he* thinks it's worth pursuing." Okay, I will admit it. I'm acting like a first-grader. But he is being Impossible.

He glares a moment longer, then beeps Marilyn on the intercom. "Marilyn, do you know where Alisha Maynor is?"

"No. Want me to page her?" she chirps back over the speaker.

"Yeah, that'd be great. Tell her to come to my office."

What is Bovano up to?

He leans back in his chair, drumming his fingers on the armrest, gazing lazily out the window and humming. He doesn't invite me to sit, so I just stand there, hands shoved into my pockets, watching him. He needs a haircut.

"Eddie, I'd like you to meet Alisha Maynor," he finally says, gesturing to the door.

"Hello, Eddie." A woman's voice drifts into the room from behind my back.

I turn. Her bright emerald eyes nearly knock me off my feet.

Chapter 23

VECTOR NINJA

Angle, angle, angle, angle.

My mind is a skipping CD as I trudge up the steps of the uptown bus like a zombie. I can't get the word out of my head. It's important somehow. Something I learned last year in that architecture and design class I took at Senate . . .

I plop down onto the hard plastic seat. The bus is only half full, thank goodness. I need quiet time to collect myself before entering my apartment and squaring off with fussy cats and inquisitive parental units.

I'm really floored about the whole Alisha thing. Turns out she's an undercover cop they placed in the operation a year ago. Bovano didn't tell me much, only that she's been posing as an art curator who is interested in making a few bucks on the side, and has been "helping" the thieves cook up a plan. According to her, she was at the Winston Café with a friend. Pure coincidence.

I'm not sure if I buy her story, but I do know this: if I put it together that Alisha is part of the case, then I am onto things, and am actually getting pretty good at this detective stuff.

I hop off the bus at my stop and walk two blocks to my apartment building. Leaves are popping on the trees, the flowery smell of spring in the air. I peel off my jacket as I go. It's warm and I should be grabbing a Frisbee and meeting Jonah in Central Park, but all I can think is *angle, angle, angle*.

Dad is in his office and Mom is on the Internet. After a quick hello to both of them, I set up shop in the privacy of my room, spreading out the marked-up city map on my desk. I root through my drawers for architecture supplies from last year's class and find a protractor, tracing paper, and triangular scales.

I line up the tools again and again. Nothing fits. Trace and retrace. Measure and angle and remeasure. Nothing. And then . . .

"No way," I say out loud. The protractor is lined up with the Neue and the Jewish Museum, the other sites falling into a pattern of angles. A perfect pattern fit for the geometric obsession of Lars Heinrich.

"NO WAY!" My cackling laughter is a little too close to a mad scientist's, but I don't care. I've done it, I've done it—I've cracked Lars's puzzle!

Grinning like a fool, I snatch the phone from my desk and dial Jonah's number.

"Look," I say to Jonah, leaning over his shoulder to draw lines through the different points on the map with a protractor. We're in his bedroom, the map and my drawing supplies laid out on his desk. He's hunched over the materials like a vulture.

I nudge him to the side so I can continue my illustrations. "If you draw lines at a thirty-, sixty-, or ninety-degree angle from each site on the map, they all intersect with the Guggenheim. The Neue Galerie and the Jewish Museum are at 180 degrees, flanking the Guggenheim on either side. Straight vectors through them. All is divisible into one eighty. Thirty, sixty, ninety." I twist the protractor around on the map, making light marks with a pencil.

"It's a special kind of right triangle," I continue. "Thirty-sixty-ninety. All lines lead to the Guggenheim."

I pause for dramatic effect, letting him absorb the information. He stares at the map, rocking in his seat.

When he doesn't comment, I add, "The cafés across the street must be meeting places. Drop-off zones for money, recon, who knows what else. They've been sending me to the wrong museums. The Guggenheim is where it's going down."

My sketch is actually quite beautiful, an intricate shower of fireworks raining down from the Guggenheim onto the city blocks.

Jonah frowns at the map. "Wow. Yeah . . . awesome," he says in a flat tone.

My eyes narrow. "You don't seem very excited." Does he understand what I'm talking about? Or is he just jealous I figured it out before he did?

He scratches his head. "Don't take this the wrong way, but it seems kind of easy."

"Easy?" I splutter. "This took me all afternoon!"

He twists in his chair to look at me while chewing on a pencil. I'm growing more and more irritated, and the three-year-old inside me hopes he bites off a piece and swallows it by accident.

"Edmund, think about Lars in Paris. How complicated that design was." He holds up his hands when I growl. "I'm not saying you're wrong. I agree with you. I think you figured it out. But what if Lars did this on purpose? What if he designed this angle thing to throw the cops off the *real* crime?"

He turns back to the map, making marks of his own. "Also, if we take Alisha into consideration with the two sites of the Winston Café and the ice cream incident, then the whole vector thing is thrown right out the window. Those two blocks are over too far, not at significant angles to the Guggenheim . . ."

I leave him mumbling in his room so I don't say something I regret. It's almost dinnertime and I'm hungry and grumpy, so I root around in his kitchen for some snacks. He has *way* better food at his house. Corn chips sprayed with a variety of flavored salts, a crunchy goodness deemed Illegal by my mother. Jonah's parents still aren't home from work. I'm hoping they'll walk in the door with Chinese food and invite me to stay.

I decide to take the high road and humor Jonah's theory. What if Lars is misleading the cops on purpose? What else could be going on here?

I stare at the bright yellow and blue tiles of the countertop while I munch on Doritos. The question we haven't been asking ourselves is, if they only steal Picassos, then why would we be at a stakeout at the

Neue and Jewish Museum? There are no Picassos there. What is Bovano thinking? I try to put myself in his shoes, get into his brain. It's an icky proposition.

The Neue Galerie contains only German and Austrian art. Picasso is from Spain. Is Lars sentimental for his homeland?

The Jewish Museum is a mystery as well. The only significant link I've come up with between Picasso and Jewish people is his famous painting *Guernica*. It depicts bombs being dropped by Nazis on a village in Spain, when the Spanish fascist government allowed Hitler to use their people as target practice. How nice of them.

Guernica is huge, though. Eleven by twenty-six feet. I'm having a hard time picturing a heist with a forklift. Plus, it's in Madrid.

I've been doing a lot of research. I may be turning into my father.

Only ten more days of school until April vacation. We have a week off, which will be spent in major lockdown trying to figure this out. It *has* to be the Guggenheim. I'll spend my entire vacation there, sleep on the floor if I have to. I wonder if I can ask to see the museum's security tapes without raising Bovano's suspicions.

Slowly I walk back to Jonah's bedroom. He's still muttering to himself and playing with my protractor, knees bouncing up and down and rattling the desk. I resist the temptation to throw my bowl of chips at his head.

I know I'm right about this. Lars is going to rob the Guggenheim, a museum full of treasure and priceless art and *a lot* of Picassos. He'll be there, I can feel it in the very depths of my skinny bones.

Now I just have to prove it.

Chapter 24

TOUCHY SUBJECTS

April 19

April vacation was a total bust. For half the time my parents dragged me to my grandma's house in New Jersey, and the other half I spent watching Jonah stew in his room, eating peanut butter out of the jar and redrawing the angle problem every two seconds. Not my best week. I even went to the Guggenheim on Friday, but without police support I couldn't pretend to be an art student (special permission only) and I had to pay admission, which set me back twenty bucks. Plus I felt weirdly exposed without Bovano there to growl at me over the IPODICU.

Only four weeks remain until the case is dropped. *Four weeks!*

Right when I start to panic about my paycheck disappearing and Senate slipping through my fingers,

I am called for my next assignment. The Guggenheim.

I want to phone Jonah and yell "Aha! Told you so!" at the top of my lungs, but that wouldn't be very classy, plus I'm in Bovano's car and he's watching me like a hawk in the rearview mirror.

The Guggenheim is an über-huge museum on Fifth Avenue, a monstrosity shaped like a cement cylinder that somehow still manages to seem beautiful despite its mass of concrete. As a modern and highly important museum, it's equipped, I'm sure, with a billion security lasers and ninjas with machine guns. To rob it takes a lot of guts and technical know-how. Pulling it off would be the heist of the century.

I step into the lobby, the glow from the skylight above warming my shoulders. The inside of the museum circles around and around in an upward spiral, with an enormous open space in the center that leads to a glass ceiling filled with geometrical panels. They form a dazzling pattern that would make Lars Heinrich drool.

Clutching my canvas and easel under my armpit, I stride toward the modernist section where the Pi-

175

cassos hang. The guard nods at me as I pass, knowing that I am Someone Important, someone not to be searched. My back is straight, my senses on high alert. This may be one of my last assignments, and I am determined to make it count.

"Eddie Red, testing," I whisper into my sleeve.

"I copy you, Eddie. Don't mess it up," Bovano responds, his usual cheerful words of encouragement.

I ignore him and get to work. Draw, look, listen, snap mental images, walk around, draw some more.

I am in the middle of imitating a Kandinsky in reds and blues when I see him.

Him.

Lars Heinrich, in the flesh. The hair pricks up on the back of my neck as if a werewolf just walked in. Is it really him? I can only see a bit of him from the side. His chin is different. His hair is black, stuffed under a baseball cap. Normally I wouldn't give him a second look, but his ear . . . his ear is the same.

I need to do something. The clock is ticking, and he isn't going to stay long. He's talking to two men I don't recognize, whispering in a group. He keeps shifting his black-gloved hands, covering the sides of his face and gesturing to the art on the wall.

I hesitate. My Marco mistake at the Neue haunts

me, making me doubt myself. I leave my canvas and walk over as casually as I can.

Bovano must see that I see him, because he starts to yammer over the IPODICU, "What are you doing, Eddie? What do you see? Just go over to the painting and then turn back. Is it that guy in the cap? He's not a perp, I don't recognize him. No, not that way. Over to your left. Your other left, Eddie! Keep your distance. Get in and out. And no yelling *Marco* for the love of—" He bites back whatever colorful thing he was about to say.

My heart is pounding like a jackhammer and I can't concentrate. Every time I get close enough to glimpse Lars, he changes position and blocks my view.

I pretend to study a painting on the wall. I move in right next to the group, my pulse exploding out my ears.

"Edmund! Not so close! You're practically on top of him! Back off now!"

Did Bovano just call me Edmund? Really? Now, of all moments? I switch off the IPODICU. I know that he's going to annihilate me, but I just can't think with his voice gnawing at my brain.

Lars's head is bent down, his hat brim pulled low. All I have is that stupid ear. I need this picture.

I tug on his sleeve, playing the overly helpful kid. "Excuse me, sir, did you drop this?" I hold out a chewed Bic pen from my pocket.

He turns toward me and then quickly looks away. "No," he snaps. I see his face for a millisecond.

Click.

Gotcha.

Sharper chin, higher cheekbones. His brow is tighter. Eyes more tapered and without wrinkles. He's had a facelift for sure. Different nose, longer and pointy. Same blue eyes, same slightly unhinged look I've seen in his picture.

It's him. No doubt about it. It's him! I slink back to my canvas while fumbling with my IPODICU. Bovano's bellowing voice invades my ear as I switch on. "—you there? Do you read me?" A string of swears. "Eddie, do you copy? Was it someone important? Talk to me!"

Staring down at my canvas, I pretend to scratch my nose. "The blond guy from the mug shot," I whisper into my sleeve mike. I can't use the name "Lars Heinrich." Bovano will know I've been snooping.

"Stay right where you are," Bovano commands in an eerily quiet voice.

I nod and glance up at the dark-haired, plastically altered Lars.

He's gone.

"You touched him? You touched him. You actually touched a suspect. Unbelievable. We have you on tape. Touched him. After all I said, all of my warnings. And you switched off your receiver! How dare you disobey my orders! You don't . . . I can't . . ."

Bovano storms around his office, sputtering out sentence fragments, buzzing like an angry hornet.

I don't know what he's so cheesed off about. I got a picture of the guy, no harm done. Just a dumb kid asking about a dropped pen. Nothing suspicious about that. And as a reward for my clever spy maneuver, I now get to enjoy the Frank Bovano motto, *Screaming Is Caring*.

"Will you ever listen to my rules?" he snarls. "They exist for YOUR safety, Eddie. *You*. I can't believe . . . You actually . . . You're going to give me a heart attack before this is over!"

I can't quite believe I touched Lars either. It was like shaking hands with a famous person. I'm still hopped up on adrenaline from the experience. I feel

NEW LARS

bad that he got away, but at least now we know what he looks like. I just drew a picture of him that sent the whole office into action. The new and improved Lars Heinrich, hair dyed, face lifted, maybe a fake nose glued on.

Bovano rumbles at me for a solid twenty minutes. "We're going to have a serious talk with the chief. You will not work here if you can't take orders. First the Neue, then the Taser, now this! What's next? Guns? Kidnapping? You almost blew the whole thing!"

I'm thinking now is not the best time to tell him that I seem to have lost my IPODICU.

Chapter 25

GAME

April 23

Four days later, my Lars victory has faded. Something just doesn't add up. Why would he have come out in the open like that? His disguise was good but he was completely exposed. What if, like Jonah thought, Lars *wants* to mislead us? If that's his plan, he's succeeded. The police are distracted, focusing all efforts on the Guggenheim. What if Lars is planning to rob something else? *Somewhere* else? What if the places where I saw Alisha—the ice cream street and the photography exhibit at the Winston Café—mean something?

Alisha acted as if it was all a coincidence. But what if the sites are clues to a hidden pattern, and she's covering for Lars? If that's true, how do I prove her involvement? I can't exactly yell, "Liar! Liar! Pants on fire!" and expect *that* to do the trick.

"I just don't get it," Jonah says as he jumps up and down on my bed. "What am I not seeing? The angle thing . . . too easy. A trap. How can this be possible? I always crack the codes. It's the meds. I've lost my edge. Not good, not good." He's in full-on rant mode.

Of course it doesn't make sense, I think, witnessing Jonah go from "active boy" to "lunatic monkey" before my eyes.

He's pinned the map up on the slanted part of my ceiling and is examining it while bouncing like a wild kangaroo. He leaps up and studies the map midair, contemplates the information as he lands on the bed, then springs back up to scrutinize it some more. This is Jonah "focusing." I'm just glad my new IPODICU is hidden, or he'd break it for sure, and Bovano would have a coronary. I barely survived our conversation about me losing the first one. Bovano turned a color that makes dark red look pale.

Up and down. Up and down.

My mom will be home in ten minutes, and then we'll both be in trouble if he doesn't cool it. Joyce Lonnrot is *not* a fan of bed jumping or lunatic monkeys.

"What's wrong with you?" I ask, not bothering to hide the annoyance in my voice. I already know the answer. I've suspected something was up the moment I opened the door to let him in.

"Off my meds. Clouding my thinking." Bounce-bounce-bounce.

"Does your mom know? That's really dangerous, Jonah. And stupid."

"Course not. Now, quiet. I need to focus . . . That museum there, plus that café there . . . Why? Why? Why? NO! There . . . and there . . ."

I haven't seen this Jonah for a while, the Jonah who can't stop speaking, the one who says anything and everything that comes into his brain.

My earliest memories are of Jonah talking incessantly. We were two, and at first my parents thought that my speech was delayed, but then they realized it was just because Jonah did all the talking for both of us. A few years after, the doctors diagnosed him with ADHD (the OCD came later on) and decided to put him on special medication, which at first doped him out but then steadied him, made him a little less hyper and impulsive. And quieter.

Unforeseen Problem #3: Best friend and trusted codetective goes off his meds.

This may lead to possible Mom interference, in which case the investigation will severely grind to a halt. I can't do it without Jonah. Don't get me wrong; I'm not a huge proponent for medicating today's youth. All I'm saying is, sometimes it helps.

"Napoleon!" he screeches, grabbing the map mid-spring and ripping it down to the bed.

"Jonah, that map belongs to my—"

"Napoleon, Edmund! Chess! Napoleon made his troops learn chess. Strategy . . . military tactics . . ." His fingers fly around on the map, tracing invisible lines and jabbering to himself once again:

"Pawn move here . . . another here. Eight squares across . . . Oh my God, Edmund! I've done it!" He grabs my shirt and I stumble forward as we both crash to the floor. My glasses fly off and go skidding across the room.

"Jonah! Ow!" I protest, shoving him off me. I start to grope around blindly on the rug. If he breaks my glasses, my parents will flip.

"No, that one doesn't fit. Not unless . . . I gotta go," he announces suddenly. "I'm taking this with me. I'll call you tonight."

He crams the map into his bag, murmuring about

185

the Internet and chess moves and a peanut butter sandwich. And then he's gone.

I finally find my glasses and look around.

A mangled bedspread. A pile of papers strewn across the floor. And silence.

What just happened?

He calls two hours later, an urgent hiss through the phone.

"Come over now, Edmund. My parents are on to me; they made me take my meds. I'm getting drowsier by the second. They're plenty mad and I have to go to a doctor, and they might switch medications, which means I am down for the count. I need to show you this . . ." His voice trails off mysteriously and the line goes dead.

With a vague excuse to my parents, I head out the door. My fingers brush the new IPODICU in my pocket. *You're not off the case yet,* I remind myself as I sprint to his apartment.

I find Jonah pacing in his room.

"Good, you're here," he says, forcing me into his desk chair. "You're not going to believe this!" He spreads the map out across the desk. It's ripped, wrinkled, and stained, and smells suspiciously of peanut butter.

"We've been studying Museum Mile at the wrong angle. With Central Park on top. That's how everyone always holds the map, right? But look what happens when we turn it upside down, and the park is at the bottom. See?"

He's waiting for me to have a moment of brilliance. It's not coming.

"Uh . . . no."

"Lars Heinrich is playing chess," he proclaims, putting his arms out in a *Ta-da!* move.

"Huh? I thought he was all about geometric patterns."

Jonah makes a scoffing noise in his throat. "Geometry is *so* eighties, Edmund. Lars is messing with the police. Fooling them into thinking it's like the job in Paris. But he's got another game going on, another pattern hidden in the city map. Chess moves. Look!" He places little cut-out chess pieces on the city blocks.

"There are two rows of eight blocks across. That's just how you set up a side in chess. The cafés are the row of pawns. Viewed as having little value. No art in them. Museum Mile has the power. The Neue and the Jewish Museum are the rooks. They anchor the board. The Guggenheim is the king. The king must be protected at all times, which is what the cops are doing."

"So then what's the game?" I say. "There aren't enough sites for many moves. Just the ice cream and the Winston. Two moves?"

"There's only one game that fits: Fool's Mate. It's the quickest game to checkmate. Each side moves two times. The Winston and the ice cream match up to the White pawn moves. One on Lexington, one on Park Ave. It's perfect!"

I rub my left temple. "That's two moves for white. What about black?"

"This move, queen to h4, is the final move of the Fool's Mate game. Black wins." He drags the queen diagonally over to a residential neighborhood on Lexington.

"What happens on that block?" I ask. "It's just some apartments. No museum there."

"Lars is after another Picasso, right? He ruled Paris in the eighties with his Picasso Gang—he'll do the same here in New York. The target doesn't have to

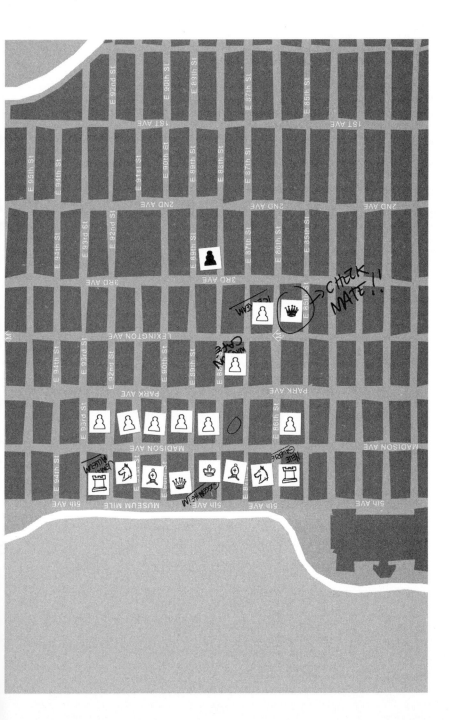

be a museum. Someone out there owns a Picasso. *In their home.*"

I'm still confused. Chess has never been my game. Probably because Jonah destroys me every time we play. "So that block is . . . ?"

His eyes wide, Jonah glances around, looking paranoid, like someone has bugged his room.

"Checkmate."

Chapter 26

RECONNAISSANCE

—

"Uh . . ." I say oh so intelligently. "Can you take me through it again?" Like I said, chess is not my game. And I need to be able to explain this to Bovano. If he'll listen to me.

Jonah sighs. "Edmund, look. Do you see the chessboard? The two rows of eight figures? Yes? Good. That's the white side of the board. The police side. Kind of. But it's also Lars. More on that in a second. So in the game of Fool's Mate, white starts the game and moves a pawn. G2 to g4. That lands on the block of your ice cream caper. Lars sent Alisha there to meet with Marco and the bald guy. They were the white pawn that day, the police pawn. Which makes sense because Alisha technically works for the police. The knife fight your Dad saw must have happened after Alisha left. The guys were probably arguing about how lame Lars is with this whole chess game thing."

He pauses to take a deep breath. I don't dare interrupt him when he's on a roll. "Then black moves," he says. "E7 to e5, up on Third Ave. That spot doesn't matter. We must have missed a meeting. No big deal. Then white moves: f2 to f3. That's the Winston. Once again Alisha was there as the white side. But Lars is pulling the strings and telling her where to go. Are you with me?"

"Okay . . . I get that."

"So then in Fool's Mate, black, or Lars and Alisha in this case, moves once more, this time queen from d8 to h4. That puts the white king in checkmate. Game over. Black wins. Lars wins."

"But if the king is the Guggenheim, isn't that still where the crime will take place? Where the attack will come?"

"No. The game ends at checkmate—it ends with the Queen over on Lexington. No need to go on once there's checkmate. And think about the symbolism: the police are fools because they're guarding the king. But the *queen* will conquer. *Alisha* is the queen. She's lying about her involvement. She has *fooled* the cops. Where she moves will be a Picasso. Lexington Avenue. Wealth. A private art collector. Game over."

It's starting to make sense. Lars is nuts, but maybe

not crazy enough to try and rob the Guggenheim. He's using it as a decoy. "But how can there be a game when the police aren't playing? They don't *know* it's chess. How can there be two sides?" A terrible thought slams into me. "Wait, does Lars know about *me?* Am I playing this game with him? Alisha knows about me, and if she told Lars, then—"

Jonah shakes his head, clucking his tongue. "Lars is playing both sides. It's his own personal game, set up just how he wants it. The police may *symbolically* be the white side, but Lars controls the whole board. He doesn't know about you. All he cares about is the game." He leans in closer, his gaze slightly wild. "He's crazy," he whisper-hisses.

I want to point out that Jonah looks a little crazy himself at the moment, but that seems counterproductive. Instead I stare at the chess pieces, letting it all sink in.

Jonah continues in a more normal voice, "It's fascinating, actually, the hidden psychology of the whole thing. Black will win, but there's a black boy working for the white team, so if we solve this and stop the crime, then white wins but with a black knight. Which is you. See the irony?"

"Jonah, I—"

"Okay, maybe a bit of a stretch. Still cool to think about. I think we should call ourselves the White Knights. Or the Black? Or the Black-and-White? What do you think?" He starts to drum on his desk and giggle.

I ignore him and inspect the map. I see the chessboard. I get it.

And I think he's right.

April 24

"I've got binoculars, a map, a phone directory, cell phone, duct tape, two peanut butter sandwiches . . . Do you want food? 'Cause those are for me," Jonah says as he packs up his camouflage backpack. He isn't groggy today, thank goodness. The meds have kicked in, his mood is stable, and we're back on track.

"No, thanks," I say. "Duct tape?"

"Yeah. Don't leave home without it. Let's go over the plan."

Our first real recon job. We have to assess the checkmate block, make sure there actually *is* a Picasso in one of the buildings before I go and assault Bovano with outrageous theories about chess and the green-eyed-lady-who-is-a-bad-guy. But even after a good night's sleep, I still don't think it sounds so far-fetched. It *feels* right.

The task: Track every face, note every apartment. Figure out who owns a Picasso. As if it's going to be that simple.

It's a beautiful spring day in Central Park. Birds are flying around and kids are running by. The smell of fresh-cut grass lingers in the air. But despite the city life around us, it's eerily quiet as we march toward our destination. All I hear is the slap of our shoes on the pavement and Jonah's weird breathing noises involving some snuffles and a *wheee-snort* every now and again. Does he always breathe this loudly and I've never noticed, or is he getting sick? Or am I just nervous about doing this?

I try to focus my mind into a chess framework, think how Lars thinks. Get inside his head. Here we are, two brave foot soldiers pushing forward, two connected pawns commencing our counterattack, establishing our outpost . . . to bind the enemy, squeeze them, pin them for a capture. I may be getting carried away with my chess metaphors here.

Think like Lars . . . think like Lars. It's hard to put yourself into the mind of a madman. Plus now I'm craving croissants and an espresso like the ones I saw in the café photos of him. Just shoot me if I start wearing black turtlenecks.

We cross Fifth Avenue (a.k.a. Museum Mile) and head over to Lexington, with its impressive glass-paned apartment buildings and expensive BMWs. Jonah nods to me and we get into position, ready to walk the block.

He clears his throat. "Black-and-White Knights, recon mission number one. Lexington side, left to right, door one has a doorman. Door two, brown-stone, private entrance. Door three, apartments, no doorman. Buzzer system."

Jonah is making me as jittery as a caffeinated cat. He stole a voice recorder from his dad and is taking "mental notes." Loudly.

I keep looking over my shoulder to see if anyone has noticed. I swear people are staring. It's like *we're* the robbers, casing the houses, registering each soul on the block. I'm waiting for the cops to show up any second.

Before I can rip the recorder out of his fingers, he grabs my arm and stuffs me behind a garbage can. He crouches down low next to me and pulls out a sandwich. Chomping away, he peers over the top of the can to get one last good look at the road. Does he think this is "undercover"? I roll my eyes. It's eleven in the morning, broad daylight. At least we just look like a couple of dumb kids.

He contemplates the street as if he's pondering the mysteries of the universe. Munching noises combined with his clogged breathing produce a symphony of squishy, moist sounds. Just when I think my nerves can't take any more, he swallows the voluminous mass of gummy butter and white bread and turns to me.

"Edmund," he says in a sticky voice. "We're going to need to go door to door. Get inside people's apartments."

There are at least five hundred families on this block, if not more. Impossible. How he's going to pull this one off, I have no idea.

Chapter 27

GIRL POWER

April 30

I might have known Jonah's plans would involve me making an idiot out of myself. He borrowed a Girl Scout uniform from a girl who goes to his temple, and is now shoving me into my parents' room to get changed.

"It's the only way, Edmund. You can totally pull it off. You're a *much* better actor than I am. And you're thin enough to fit into the dress. All you need is a wig, which I know your mother has from last Halloween. People love the Girl Scouts. You'll be inside their apartments in no time!"

"Why can't we do your pizza idea?" I whine.

He gives me an incredulous look. "And buy five hundred pizzas? Cookies are where it's at. It's the *promise* of future cookies that gets you in the door.

Chocolate, mint, coconut, peanut butter . . ." His eyes glaze over, fantasizing about peanut butter cookies. He's a total addict. Shaking the image from his head, he stuffs the uniform into my hands and firmly closes the door. "Now, change!" he demands.

I groan and strip out of my clothes. The dress slides on easily, a perfect fit. It's unbelievably itchy and hot. What cruel person decided wool was a good idea? I have a newfound respect for girls and their wardrobe sufferings.

From behind the door Jonah jabbers at me about our mission. He's made a list of the properties we're going to hit, prioritizing them on probability of success: "The wealthiest-looking buildings first. Apartments with a buzzer system. Then brownstones. Doormen are last. Avoid doormen at all costs."

He claims it's a system based on statistics, but I know it's because he's scared of doormen. He broke a vase in his building's lobby once, and Grigore the doorman went postal on him. Now whenever we walk through to get to Jonah's apartment, Grigore starts muttering in Romanian and gesturing to the new vase in the lobby. Post-traumatic vase syndrome.

The Girl Scout uniform is on and the mirror tells all: Right now I look like a skinny cross-dresser who was attacked by a swarm of mosquitos. I can't stop scratching at the horrible material.

Itching away, I dig through my mom's stuff in the closet, locating her long brown wig under some sweaters. Last year she went as Beyoncé to a costume party, and literally stopped traffic.

"Are you done yet?" Jonah's muffled voice calls from the other side of the door.

"Just a minute," I grumble. Why do *I* have to be the guinea pig? Then I see myself with the wig on. Jonah's right; I *do* look like a girl.

Terrific.

I pin the hair back with one of my mom's hairclips. *Not bad,* I think, turning to the side and checking out my new look. I am innocent. A sweet, geeky girl, perfect to let into your house and catalog your most expensive possessions.

I open the door. Jonah stands there, eyes bulging out. A strange noise gurgles in his throat. Clutching his pants, he turns on his heel and sprints down the hallway. I hear the bathroom door slam, followed by peals of laughter. He better not have peed on the floor mid run.

As his laughter continues, I sigh and take off the wig. Back to the drawing board.

May 7
"Did you switch meds?"

"No," Jonah yawns in a cotton-filled voice. "I think I'm getting sick." He puts down his binoculars to blow his nose. We're out on Lexington Ave. again, crouched behind the same stupid trash can.

Great. The clock is ticking, he's getting sick, and we have an über-lame plan to find the Picasso. Of course, I couldn't come up with a better idea, so I can't complain.

We're pretending to be students doing a survey about art in the city, complete with questionnaires, clipboards, and paper coffee cups. (The last prop is for *effect*. According to Jonah, people who do surveys are up all night performing caffeinated number crunching.)

Jonah thinks it's a brilliant plan. "Why not just ask people, point-blank, *Do you own a Picasso?*" he says as we begin to walk the block. "They'll think it's normal. Why would we, two young kids, be checking out their homes for robbery? They won't think of it. They'll believe us, trust me."

This is getting us nowhere fast. How many people live on this block? Eight hundred? A thousand? And who wants to talk to some coffee-drinking kids about art?

After climbing a set of stone steps, Jonah rings the first apartment on the list, pressing the buzzer with purpose. I stay back a few stairs, my heart beating fast. We're actually doing this. No turning back now.

"What are you boys doing?" An elderly lady with purplish hair and a turquoise silk scarf is glowering at us from the sidewalk. Her wrinkled face is pinched with suspicion.

"Excuse me, ma'am," Jonah says in a smarmy voice. "We are students doing an art survey for our history class. May we have a moment of your time, please?"

"No, you may not. Now leave these steps at once or I will call the police!" She huffs by me up to the landing, brandishing a key like she's holding a knife. Jonah touches her arm. Big mistake.

"Unhand me, you ruffian!" she screeches, whapping him over the head with her purse.

"Ow!" he yelps, stumbling down the stairs. The woman slams the door with gusto. This time I'm the one who loses it laughing.

"What are we going to do now?" asks Jonah, rubbing his head, a pout forming on his face. He sits down on the bottom step like a dejected puppy dog.

"I don't know," I manage to pant out. Tears are running down my cheeks. I can't stop laughing.

Jonah glares at me.

A middle-aged brunette woman is strolling toward us on the sidewalk. She pauses, and tilts her head to one side. "Is there a problem, boys?" She has a pleasant smile and is wearing large pearls that could probably pay for Senate. One for every year.

I collect myself, for Jonah's sake. "My friend and I are trying to do an art survey for class, and a lady from this building just hit him with her purse." I gesture in the direction of Jonah, who's still massaging his curly red dome. Looking quite pitiful, I might add.

She chuckles. "You must have met Matilda Swayne. Mean old bag, isn't she? No pun intended. I live here as well." She gestures to the fancy apartments. "What sort of survey are you doing? Maybe I can help."

Jonah brightens. "We're doing a project about private art ownership. Asking people if they have any famous works in the family, like a Picasso for example."

"I don't own anything like that," she says. "But the lady that hit you? She's got three Picassos. So I hear.

She doesn't ever let anyone in her place. Just yells at us if we dare to walk by her door."

Jonah turns to grin at me.

Three Picassos?

I've said it before and I'll say it again: If you're a kid and you want to solve a police investigation, you need a boatload of dumb luck.

Chapter 28

CLOGGED

May 9

I have to wait two whole days to see Bovano, since yesterday was Sunday and we went to my grandma's for a Mother's Day lunch. She makes the best chocolate cake in the world. I start salivating even thinking about it.

But now it's back to work, back to reality. Back to the police station.

"I need to speak with him," I tell Marilyn. "Please tell him it's urgent."

Bovano is in his office with the blinds drawn and is refusing to see me. Marilyn isn't cooperating either. She's standing at her desk, edging toward Bovano's door as if she'll block it if need be. I guess she's still a little wary about the time I ran by her and barged into his office. I hope Bovano didn't yell at her about it.

"Eddie, he's in a meeting right now, hon. Just leave your message with me and I'll make sure he gets it." She pulls a pen from behind her ear, ready to jot down a note.

What do I say? *Hey, Detective Bovano, I snuck a peek at your case files and I think you've got it all wrong. And I still think your cop friend Alisha is in on it. And there are three unguarded Picassos where you're not looking.*

He'll kill me for sure.

"Thanks, Marylin," I mumble, turning away. "I'll try him again tomorrow."

One week till it's all over. End game.

May 10
Jonah's mom calls before school on Tuesday. He's über-sick and is on antibiotics. She wants me to get his schoolwork.

> Unforeseen Problem #4: Best friend and codetective is down for the count with a sinus infection.

At school I'm lonely and itching to talk about the case. Plus I've come to realize that not only does Jonah provide entertaining dialogue and amusing antics, but he is also my own personal bully buffer. It's not something I'm proud of.

The strike comes sixth period, just outside the science classroom.

"Hey, Edmund, where's your girlfriend?" the troll grunts, grabbing the cap off my head.

"Hey!" I yell in my firm voice. The one my dad taught me.

"Hey, what?" Robin steps closer. The kid is a wall of beef. My dad didn't tell me what to do after the firm voice thing. That was supposed to take care of the situation, not make it worse.

Up close, I can see that Robin Christopher has really weird facial hair, tufts of blond accentuating the red blotches on his skin. I can't believe he's got a beard at our age. Must be eating too many hormone-injected hamburgers.

I have no plan. I tremble a little and eyeball my hat in his hand. I want that cap.

Mr. Pee rescues me. "Robin, is that Edmund's hat?" he asks as he hustles us into the classroom.

"Yeah. I was just checkin' it out." Robin sneers at me and throws the hat by my feet when we've lost Mr. Pee's attention.

I understand now why Jonah hasn't told anyone about the abuse. Intimidation stinks.

I walk to the station after school, bully aggravation churning in my veins. I'm not sure why, but now seems like the right time to confront Bovano. Blitz chess is on. I have nothing to lose.

I catch Bovano by the water cooler.

"What do you want, Eddie?" he grumbles at me while lumbering back to his cave with windows. "The case is being dropped next week."

"I know, Detective, and I really need to speak with you. And I need you to listen."

I follow him into his office. He sees me enter, and sighs. "You have two minutes. Don't test my patience."

We both sit. I'm happy that his large desk is between us. Where to begin?

"I have proof that Alisha is part of the crime."

"Eddie, *no*. Get out. Do your parents know where you are?"

"I know about the geometric shapes on the map, Detective. I know that Lars Heinrich is planning a crime like the one in Paris."

"How did you . . . Have you been looking through my files?"

"The map is in plain sight." I gesture to the wall with my hand. "And you used the name Lars Heinrich at dinner."

He starts to speak and then stops, mouth opening and closing like a confused guppy's. He wants to yell at me, but realizes he may have slipped up. Of course, I don't mention that he only used the name "Lars."

When he finally speaks, his voice is low and shaky, stifling the anger he desperately wants to unleash on me. "Eddie, there are things going on that you have no idea about. We have a lot of people working the situation. You gonna be a Boy Scout and try to solve it? I'm going to call your parents right now. You are way past overstepping your role here."

"I know that the markers on the map form thirty-, sixty-, and ninety-degree angles with the Guggenheim. And that all vectors lead to the Guggenheim. That's where you think the robbery will take place."

"What? That is *confidential* information! Did you break into the chief's office? How—"

"I have my people too. We figured it out. And we think it's a setup." I pull out my crinkled peanut butter map and smooth it out on his desk to show him the proof. "But the angles pattern is wrong. The real crime is on a civilian block. It's a chess game, Detective. Involving Alisha and the Winston Café . . . she's a part of the Picasso Gang."

Bovano goes nuclear with rage. "That gang name was in a CLOSED FILE. NOT ON A WALL OR INVENTED IN SOME TWEEN THINK TANK. YOU HAVE BEEN SNOOPING IN MY DESK!!!"

He stands and clumps toward me, hands shaking like he *will* choke the life out of me right here, right now.

"No, you can't prove that," I stammer, leaping from my chair and hustling backwards until my back presses against the office door. My panicked fingers grapple to find the doorknob. I make contact.

"YOU STEAL FILES FROM ME, TELL YOUR BUDDIES ABOUT THE CRIME, ABOUT BE-ING EDDIE RED! YOU'RE FIRED!" he thunders. "GET OUT!!"

I twist the knob, shove my shoulder hard into the wooden panel, and run. This definitely qualifies as an "always run" Nike defense situation.

I can't call getting fired an Unforeseen Problem. I guess I saw it coming a mile away.

So much for a blitz.

Chapter 29

FRIDAY

May 13

It takes me three days to work up the courage to go back to the station. I need Bovano to listen to me, and I'm hoping he's cooled down by now. Jonah agrees it's a good idea— although he's still really sick and spaced out from the cold medication he's taking, so he may not be thinking clearly.

In hindsight, I should have just stayed in bed. Today is Friday the thirteenth. Never do *anything* on that day.

All day in class I pump myself up to have the guts to enter the station after school, all for nothing. Frank Bovano isn't here; his office is dark and abandoned.

I need to try one more time to reach him. Maybe if I leave him a voice message, he'll actually listen. He needs to know Matilda Swayne's address. I don't think it was legible on the map I left for him. If I give him the information, then my conscience is clean. *He'll* be the one at fault if something goes down.

"Hi, Marilyn," I say, approaching her desk. She gives me a tentative nod, hand nervously fiddling with the glasses that hang on a chain around her neck. I'm sure she knows what happened a few days ago in his office. Bovano's voice almost shattered the windows.

"Can you call Detective Bovano for me and tell him I need to speak to him? I have new information about the case. I fear for his safety."

I give her my winning I'm-just-an-innocent-kid smile. Like my mom, she falls for it hook, line, and sinker.

I pretend to be very interested in the gray spotted tile beneath my feet, and then sneak a quick peek as her pink polished fingernails move over the phone pad.

She leaves a message for him. Voice mail.

"Thanks, Marilyn," I say, shaking her hand. "It's been nice working with you."

"Keep in touch, Eddie. Come back and visit us." She sniffles a little. Sweet, dependable Marilyn.

Mentally digesting the ten-digit number I saw her

press, I head out to the street and call him from my cell phone.

"Detective Bovano, it's me, Edmund . . . Eddie. Please don't delete this message. Don't get mad at Marilyn, either. She didn't give me your phone number. I figured it out myself. I'm sorry that I snooped in your office. I just wanted to help. But there are some Picasso paintings and an old lady who might be in danger."

I tell him Matilda's name and address. "I'm going there right now. I need to speak with her, get her to hear me. Maybe she'll move the paintings to a storehouse or something. Go and stay with her kids for a while."

I hesitate. What else do I have to say to this man?

"If my theory is correct, then Alisha is in on it. I'm sorry, Detective. I know you don't want to hear that. And I hope it's not true."

More pausing.

"Thanks . . . and I'm sorry."

I hang up. It's his move.

I trudge over to Lexington, worry weighing down each step I take. What if I'm wrong? What if her Picassos are completely safe and I have violated her privacy and Bovano's as well? What will Bovano do? Will he tell my parents? Of course he will, and at high volume. How can I look them in the eye after that? Will he arrest me? Make me do community service?

I should have kept my big mouth shut and just been a camera like he wanted.

A strange twitch in my neck causes me to look up as I approach Matilda's building. A pang of warning. Marco—the *real* Marco this time—is jogging up the stairs dressed as a painter in white overalls, his stringy hair tied back in a braid. Followed by Jackie Vincent and the bald man. And last but not least, the elusive Lars Heinrich. It's the *Picasso Gang*, in living color. Dressed in painter's gear.

Quickly I duck into an alley, undetected.

Into an alley.

Chapter 30

ALLEY PIPES

My first time in an alley. The circumstances could be better, but it's actually not so bad. Not evil, or even smelly. Just quiet, like an abandoned path that's poorly lit. The late-afternoon sun is falling fast, the alleyway blanketed in cool shadow. It would almost be peaceful if my nerves weren't exploding. I glue my shaking fingers to my phone in a death grip as I pull it from my pocket. *You will not drop the phone like last time.* I pause. Bovano or 9-1-1?

The 9-1-1 people will believe me. They will have to come.

"Eddie," a voice says softly behind me and I jump out of my skin. A gentle voice. A feminine voice.

"Alisha!" I say in the brightest, most non-freaked-out tone I can muster. "Wow! What a strange coincidence seeing you in an alley! My grandma lives in this building and she lost her cat and I was just calling to tell her that I can't find Sparkles anywhere!" I motion to the corridor with my open cell phone. "Oh, and have *you* seen a black and white cat with a striped tail? No? Hmm. Well, I'll have to put up posters."

My brain has officially disconnected from my mouth, but I think she's buying it. I am famous in my family for having the worst poker face in the world; just last month my grandmother took me to the cleaners in a game that cost me ten bucks. Nice little old lady, my foot. I'm hoping Alisha doesn't play cards.

She hasn't said a word. I feel the urgent need to infect the silence with more inane chatter:

"All right, well, I guess I'll be seeing you down at the station. I mean, I guess not, 'cause I got fired and I don't work there anymore and I have *nothing* to do with police business. But maybe I'll see you at another art show." A strange, nervous twitter escapes my mouth. *Time to go, Edmund.*

Alisha blinks those big green eyes at me, like she's not computing what's going on here. I seize the opportunity. "I've got to get back to my grandma's. Great to see you, Alisha." I turn to go. Ten paces to daylight and safety. I'm almost there.

The sound of a gun clicks and I freeze mid step.

"Eddie," she says in a quiet voice. "I don't believe you."

I hate poker. And chess, too, come to think of it.

She whips me around to face her nice, shiny gun. "I'll take that," she says, ripping the phone from my hands. I let her have it without a struggle, cringing away from the weapon.

She lowers the pistol slightly, eyes flitting around the cramped space as if Bovano's going to jump out from the shadows any second now.

Nope, it's just me.

Her shoulders relax, along with her pistol-packing arm. "Don't worry, Ed. I like you. But you will seriously ruin my day if you interfere. So I'm going to tie you up. Now be a good boy and come here. Don't test me, Eddie. I *will* hurt you if I have to."

A moment of brilliance enters my mind before terror snuffs out any other coherent thoughts. *Turn on your IPODICU, Edmund.* I manage to flip it on inside my pocket before she drags me away. She's freakishly strong, but I don't put up a fight. She does have a gun, after all.

Pulling me back even farther into the alley, she

calmly pulls out a roll of duct tape. Of course. Probably number two in the bad-guy survival kit. The first on the list would be a gun. Maybe a ski mask for number three. I wonder if this was what Jonah had in mind when he brought duct tape on our recon missions.

"Give me your arms," she demands. I hold my hands out in front of me and she winds the tape around and around my wrists, then anchors me to a section of drainpipe. I'm glad I have on a long-sleeved shirt, because this tape would take off several layers of skin otherwise.

The metal supports on the pipe are nailed into the brick wall, making it impossible for me to slide my arms down and off the end of the pipe. I'm stuck in a standing position, my wrists and the drainpipe connected in a tangle of gray sticky bonds.

She likes you . . . She said she likes you. She won't hurt you.

I watch her while she's laboring away, really stare at her to try to see what's going on in her mind. Does she have it in her to kill me? She's sweating, her forehead creased in determination to glue me to the pipe. A strand of brown hair falls into her eyes; she flicks it away impatiently. If it weren't for those green eyes, she'd be a bit on the mousy side. Vanilla. Librarian. But the librarians always get you in the end, don't they . . .

She stops taping me and steps back, surveying her handiwork. I'm not going *anywhere*. She ponders me for a moment. "How'd you figure it out?" she asks.

"Chess moves," I reply, trying not to let my voice shake.

"Hm . . . clever boy. And does Bovano know about our little chess game?"

I hesitate, which is not good because that just makes it look like I'm lying. I go for broke:

"Yes, but he doesn't believe me. And I won't tell anyone anything, Alisha. Please, if you just let me go . . ." Dread seizes me. Alone and left for dead in an alley? All sorts of horrible images flash though my mind: drug dealers, gang members, rats gnawing at my eyeballs, cats . . . Oh, no, cats! Angry alley cats bent on revenge after the Taser incident!

Her gaze rakes over me, the emerald in her eyes a cold laser beam. Then she leans in. I flinch. She rips off one more piece from the roll and tapes my mouth. I hyperventilate, tugging at my wrist bonds while gasping through my nose. I'm glad I don't have Jonah's sinus infection, because I'd either be covered in snot or plain dead from not being able to breathe.

I can feel tears building. Alisha pats my face and makes *shooshing* noises like I'm a toddler. She's just making it worse. I try to pull away but she traps my face between her hands and plucks off my glasses. "There," she says, placing them on the ground out of my reach. "Now you can't be a material witness."

I blink and squint, but the alley is a blur of black and brown. I'm blind as a bat, completely helpless.

"I suppose you want to know why I did it," she whispers.

I shake my head hard. I want *no* part of her alley-way confession. No information whatsoever. People with information Die.

She ignores my flailing. "I was always a good cop, always saying no while others said yes to the bribes. I looked the other way while everyone got richer around me. Except for your Bovano, of course. *He'd* never take a bribe. Not Frank Angelic Bovano." She says his name scornfully. It seems I'm not the only one on the outs with the detective.

I am trying to block my ears by squinching my eyes closed. Obviously, not working.

She drones on, amusing herself with her little speech about how she fell in love with Lars and the world of art and all the money she can make off this deal. It's like I'm in a cheesy police movie. Except this movie might jump off the screen and shoot me.

"It was Lars's idea for the chess moves," she says, tapping a finger to her chin. "He's so obsessed with playing games. You have no idea what it's like to be around someone so focused, so fixated on one particular thing."

I think of Jonah and his military obsession. *Lady, you* have no idea.

She sighs. "So you see, Eddie, it was all for love." She leans in closer, setting off a rash of goose bumps on my neck. "Love of money, that is." She chuckles. I fail to see the humor.

"I have business to attend to," she announces as if we're at a board meeting or out to coffee. "I'll be back to check on you. And if you're good, maybe I'll let you live." She tugs on my bonds to see if they'll hold, and leaves.

Massive panic attack.

I spaz out and yank on the duct tape, back and forth, back and forth, trying to rip the drainpipe away from the wall. After several pathetic attempts, I stop. The only thing I'm accomplishing is giving myself sore arms and a headache. I calm my breathing, assessing the situation:

I am taped to a drainpipe in an alley by a cop-turned-criminal. I can't see farther than my hand in front of me. Yep, that's about all I can handle assessment-wise right now. The other stuff is entirely too scary to even contemplate.

Jonah would be disappointed. He'd expect me to come up with some kind of brilliant Houdini maneuver, like cutting my bonds with a paper clip or enticing an alley rat with some spare peanut butter to chew through the tape.

Did Bovano get my phone call? Did he have his IPODICU receiver turned on? Does it even work if he's not close by? Probably not. You know things are bad when you pray that Detective Bovano will come rescue you, knowing full well that he will strangle you afterward for breaking every Bovano Rule in the book.

The logical side of my brain kicks in. *You're in a nice neighborhood, Edmund. No one's going to hurt you. There are no rats, no drug dealers. Just sweet little old ladies who have a lot of money, lethal purses, and expensive Picassos. Someone will find you on their way out to do errands. Or Alisha will make good on her promise and come check on you. She'll see that you're cooperating and will decide to let you go. Now settle down, think, and live through the next hour.*

I calm down. Time passes slowly. My arms fall asleep and my legs are twitching from standing in the same spot. I actually start to get a little bored.

Bang!

A clattering noise sends my heart rate through the roof. I twist my head from side to side but all I see are dark, blurry shadows.

Clank, bang!

Squinting my useless eyes, I am desperate to find the source of the sound. The noise comes closer with a soft shuffle. It's definitely human footsteps. I pray it's not Lars. I don't think he's a very stable individual.

The person is right next to me.

Close enough for even me to see.

I blink. There, with an unusually concerned expression on his face, stands Detective Frank Bovano.

Chapter 31

SHOTS

———

"Are you okay, Eddie?" he asks, removing the tape from my mouth and cutting my bonds with a pocket-knife. He squats down by me and pats my back, his furry eyebrows crinkled together in worry.

"You're not hurt, are you? Let me see your arms." He inspects me with the lightest of touches, and then straightens my red cap like a father would for his son.

It's like I've stepped into the Twilight Zone.

"My glasses," I say, pointing to the area where Alisha placed them. He bends down and picks them up. Not even a scratch.

"Who did this to you?" he asks.

"Alisha." The name hangs there like a big fat I-told-you-so.

"Did you see anyone else?"

"I saw Marco go into the building dressed as a

painter. He's with the other three suspects. The Picasso Gang." I might as well use their code name. No more secrets, no more lies.

Bovano nods, absorbing the information. "All right, Eddie, this is what we're going to do. You—"

A noise cuts him off, which stinks because I'm sure the plan would have involved an Evacuation of the Child, which I could truly go for right about now.

Bovano whips around, shielding me with his body.

Alisha is back with her gun raised, but not before Bovano has lifted his own pistol. A standoff, and we're trapped. It dawns on me that with two guns drawn, things could get very ugly.

I slide behind him, grateful that he is such a large guy. I take back every bad thought I've ever had about him. This man wants to protect me, I sense it with every ounce of my puny, shaking body. He *will* protect me, take a bullet for me, even.

"Drop the gun," he commands. "It's over, Alisha."

She laughs. "Next you'll tell me there's a SWAT team waiting down the block. You didn't believe the kid. Nobody did."

I hear her gun cock with a *click*. Petrified, I bury my face into Bovano's jacket. It smells like spaghetti sauce, I'm not even joking.

"Let him go, Alisha. Then it's just you and me. Let Eddie leave the alley."

I peek around his arm just a little bit so I can see Alisha's reaction. Will she consider letting me go? That would be *awesome*.

She's smiling. A very evil, very I-am-not-a-nice-person smile. "Eddie's my leverage. You don't want a dead kid on your conscience, do you, Frank?"

Detective Bovano stiffens.

"Drop the gun," she says. "Or I shoot. The boy."

I am thrilled that she has to clarify who her target is. Very comforting.

Bovano drops the gun.

There's the sound of an engine firing up. Alisha hesitates, then takes off running.

Bovano scoops up his gun and sprints after her, yelling, "Stay where you are!"

I'm not sure if that's supposed to be directed at me or Alisha, but I take him at his word.

Crouching behind a garbage can, I am safe in the alley. Safe-ish, anyway. How ironic.

A shot is fired. Squealing wheels. More shots and then the horrible sound of screeching metal and shattered glass.

I jump up and sprint for the street. I don't want to,

but my feet are in charge, and they zip me out of the alley faster than you can say "Italian in peril." I know this is not what Bovano had in mind when he said "Always run," but my partner needs my help.

A van has crashed into a light post, the driver's door open and abandoned. Alisha and the others are nowhere to be seen.

Detective Bovano is lying on the sidewalk, facedown. I run to him, yelling "Detective! Detective!"

Is he dead? It's all my fault. I crouch down, managing to roll him over with my adrenaline-spiked arms. He moans. Thank goodness. Dead people don't moan. Unless they're zombies, and don't even get me started on that scenario.

I reach into my pocket for my cell phone but then remember that Alisha took it from me. "Help!" I yell. Where is everyone? I can't believe there was a loud car crash and no one has come running. That's city noise for you.

A growing spot of blood under Bovano's jacket catches my eye. I push the leather coat back to reveal a dark red stain on his right shoulder. Not near his heart, at least. I peel off my top shirt, wad it up and apply pressure like we learned in health class. I check his vitals, counting with my watch. His color is like blanched spaghetti. The blood like tomato sauce. Now I'm thinking like an Italian, and that wigs me out even more.

Focus!

Last year in health class, we went from stop-drop-and-roll and eat-your-veggies boredom to first-aid-for-Jonah-Schwartz in the course of a week. They claim it was time for a new curriculum, but the change came on the heels of Jonah's piercing his leg with a pair of scissors. So we learned about wounds and pulses and blood flow instead. It's a good thing, too, because this year Jonah sliced his hand open on a paper cutter (what moron left that sitting out in the classroom, I have no idea).

Bovano moans again. His jacket flops open, revealing something small and silver on the inside pocket. A cell phone. I fish it out with my blood-soaked fingers. This time, I make the call.

It's hard to talk on the phone and tend to his shoulder at the same time. The blood isn't stopping like it's supposed to. After I tell the 9-1-1 operator where we are, I drop the phone to the sidewalk and press on the wound even harder, leaning on it with both hands and all my minuscule weight.

"It's okay, Detective," I say, trying to distract him.

He's semiconscious and beginning to thrash a bit. "Stay still. Help is on its way. Try to relax. Think of something nice." *But not my mother,* I mentally add.

He groans and shifts his arm. More blood bubbles out of his shoulder. "Detective, don't move," I say. "Please just breathe. Relax. Think of happy things. Like ice cream . . . or calzones."

I am an idiot.

Chapter 32

EDMUND

May 14

I give a tentative tap on the door of the hospital room the next morning.

"Come in," a low voice murmurs.

I look back at my dad. He frowns and nods me forward with his head. He still isn't speaking to me. Way too angry. He sits down in the waiting room with my mother, who is shooting me major daggers. I am on my own with this one.

I won't bore you with the gory details of what happened when they got to the station last night. Full-on wrath. Grounded until I'm eighty.

Bovano's lying on the hospital bed, his arm in a sling. A hint of flesh reveals itself through an opening in his hospital gown. I shudder at the possible sight of white hairy skin. Did they have to shave him for surgery? That must have taken hours.

Mom insisted I bring flowers. I feel like a complete tool handing him a bouquet of carnations. I should have brought pizza. White and red flowers don't seem to say "Gee, I'm sorry I got you shot." Then again, neither does pizza. Hallmark should look into a greeting card for that one.

I stand there while he raises the bed to a sitting position. The longest twenty seconds of my life.

Time to apologize to this man yet again. I gulp back my nerves. *He took a bullet for you. You owe him.* "I'm so sorry, Detective Bovano. I didn't mean to . . ."

My voice trails off. Didn't mean to what? Lie? Steal? Go behind everyone's back? Bovano still got shot in the end. *Sorry* doesn't even begin to cover it.

"Sit down, Eddie." He gestures to the chair next to his bed, his face set in a soft expression. At least I think it's a soft expression. Could be drug-induced.

Staring down at my sneakers, I slide into the seat. The low rumble of an infomercial on the television promises a magical machine that can make healthy shakes out of anything, including the living room rug. It's hypnotic.

Bovano's voice breaks my trance. "You understand now why I never wanted you on the case, don't you?

Too dangerous, too risky. When Alisha pulled the gun on you last night, I thought . . ." He shakes his head, his eyes haunted.

He clears his throat. "But I'm proud of you, kiddo. You did what I couldn't. You solved the case and stuck to your guns, even when I fired you. I'm proud of you."

We are back in the Twilight Zone from yesterday.

I want to tell him about Jonah, give credit where credit is due, but why remind him of all the rules I broke? This once, I keep my mouth shut.

"Of course," Bovano continues in a sterner tone, "I'd also like to wring your neck, but I can't. My arm's in a sling."

I let out a sound between a gasp and a giggle. I don't think he's kidding.

He studies me a moment. "I suppose you want to know what happened with the Picasso Gang? Who we caught . . . and who we didn't?"

What? They weren't all caught? My nod is shaky as it dawns on me that I may not be safe. Will they put me in a witness protection program? Cart me off to Nebraska? So much for doing all of this to stay at Senate Academy.

"We caught Alisha. And Galen Lee."

Who? My eyebrows fold in confusion.

"The guy with the long beard," he clarifies. "The Asian."

Ah, Marco. Not sure I can get used to thinking of him as Galen.

"Lars and the others are still at large. I'm guessing we won't hear from them for a while. Lars must be stunned that we figured out his elaborate game. Or that *you* did, I should say."

Bovano starts to pick at the sheet on his bed. I grip the metal armrests of my chair, the reality of the situation flooding down on me like an ice-cold shower. What if Lars knows who I am? What if he comes after me? What if—?

"You'll have to testify, Eddie. Against Alisha and Galen. You are a key eyewitness."

My breathing hitches and my leg starts to twitch.

He smiles and pats my arm. "A closed testimony. You won't be in the courtroom. They'll never see you. They don't know your real name, either. Alisha never had access to it. She'll be locked away for a very long time. Not to worry. And she swore last night on a lie-detector test that the others knew nothing about you.

She never thought you were a threat. So that's a good thing."

I settle down a little. Suddenly I have a great appreciation for Bovano's rules. Having a code name was an über-good idea.

He scrutinizes me for a moment, a sour look growing on his features like the meds are wearing off and he's just remembered how much I annoy him. "I suppose you should go. Thanks for the flowers."

I nod and stand to leave. The safety (and anger) of my parents is right outside that door. I just want to be home; being grounded is fine by me.

"Eddie?" Bovano calls from his bed.

I turn. "Yeah?"

"I'll make sure you get that check. For the full amount. You've earned it. You need the best education you can get. We need minds like yours on the force."

I am stunned. "Thanks, Detective," I whisper. Should I hug him?

No.

I think about shaking his hand, but he's staring out the window. *Just go, before he takes back his offer.* I shift to leave again.

"Edmund," he says. I freeze in the doorway.

He pauses, eyeballing me, but not in his usual I-could-eat-you-for-breakfast way.

"Thanks," he says softly, picking up the remote control and focusing his attention once more on the television.

Chapter 33

THE END?

May 16

Back at school I am feeling extremely heroic, only I can't tell anyone of course (except Jonah, who is finally out of his sinus coma). He's pretty bummed that he wasn't a part of the final showdown, but I'm glad he was sick in bed, because he could have been shot. Scratch that. He *would* have been shot.

It doesn't matter that I can't tell anyone about my weekend. My head is higher, my back straighter, my chest stronger. I may have grown a few inches.

I clean up my area in art class, carefully sliding my paintings and drawings into a folder. The familiar earthy smell of pottery clay puts a permagrin on my face. It's not a *goodbye*. It's a *see you next year*.

"Edmund?" Jenny Miller's voice startles me out of my happy thoughts.

"Yeah?" I say, like the smooth talker I am.

"I have something for you. Have a good summer."
She hands me another present. A quick glance reveals
that it's a bumper sticker, and it says something about
a cat. My brow furrows as I take it from her. Is the
girl of my dreams trying to change me? Force me to
be someone I'm not? Force me to . . . like cats?

I straighten my glasses, and then I see it correctly:
I LIKE CATS. THEY TASTE LIKE CHICKEN. I beam at her.
She smiles and waves goodbye.

I float all the way to Spanish class.

Somewhere in the middle of cloud nine, I hear
sounds coming from the boys' bathroom. Distress
noises. I walk in and there's Jonah, pinned against
the wall by our class thug. Jonah is whimpering and
his mouth is curling in a weird way, as if "Puddles" is
going to pay a visit.

"Beat it, Edmund. This is between me and your
girlfriend," Robin rumbles in my direction.

"No."

"What did you say?" He drops Jonah and turns,
eyes narrowing.

I could run. The door is right behind me. I could
run and get a teacher.

Sorry, Detective Bovano. I'm not running this
time. This guy I can take.

"Nobody makes Jonah pee his pants except me!" I yell, shoving Robin as hard as I can. He stumbles back onto a urinal and gets his sleeve wet. Gross. His face blotches up even more as he struggles to his feet.

"You're dead, loser," he jeers, clenching his fists and lunging at me. I stand my ground and do the cool leg-sweeping move that Bovano leveled me with. I've been practicing.

Robin sees me coming and tries to jump my leg. Apparently I move as slowly as my grandmother. But he stumbles and falls, this time hard on his knee. "Ahhh!" he cries out in pain.

Okay, the move didn't go as planned. But it still counts.

"Boys! What's going on here?"

Mr. Pee, impeccable timing as always.

"Thanks," sniffs Jonah. He blows his nose for the millionth time. Poor kid is still a little sick.

"No problem. Sorry about the pee comment. It came out the wrong way."

"It's all right. I know what you meant."

We're sitting outside the principal's office, awaiting our punishment. I'm not worried. But Robin Christopher should be.

Jonah reaches for another tissue. "You know, I think I'm going to give up on my military studies. It didn't prepare us for battle properly. I'm on to other things now."

"Yeah?"

"Ninjas. Much better in alleys. Sneakier."

He taps his foot, his mind going a million clicks per second. "We'll start with fencing. Nunchucks, black suits, soft quiet shoes . . . and if you're locked away in your apartment this summer, I'll scale the wall ninja-style. You're only two floors up. We'll need carabiners, climbing chalk, a harness, and rope. Think you could rig up a pulley system from your window? And throwing stars. Of course, it's summer, so there's the daylight factor . . ."

I smile and shake my head as he rattles on.

"The principal will see you now. Are you boys ready?" the secretary asks over her glasses.

Jonah turns a bit pale as we stand up. I pat him on the back. "It's okay, Jonah. We're ready," I say.

Turns out being Eddie Red is pretty great, despite the alleyway abductions, the shootouts, and the large and irritable detectives. I've got a great best friend, a present in my pocket from a cute girl, and a bully on the run. I've foiled the plans of an Evil Mastermind. I have a check in the bank to pay for Senate next year. I'm about to have a very enlightening conversation with the school principal on his bullying policies. And from the sounds of it, I have an extremely entertaining summer ahead of me.

Things are good.

In fact, they're über-good.

THE END

HOW TO DRAW FACES

1.

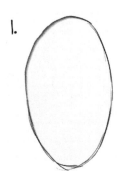

Draw with a pencil because you'll be erasing . . . a LOT!! Start by drawing an oval that tapers at the bottom, kind of like an egg.

2.

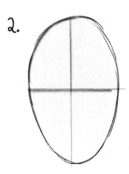

Next divide the egg in half, both vertically and horizontally with two lines.

5.

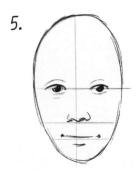

Next are the eyes. The top horizontal line goes right through their center. A good rule is to leave one eye width between them so the eyes aren't too close together or too far apart. Unless you're drawing a Cyclops and the center eye IS the eye. ALSO, the eyes are in sockets, so you need to shade behind them or they'll look weird, like they're popping off the page in surprise.

6.

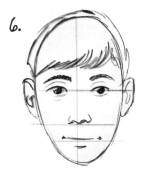

Ears are next – line them up between the bottom of the nose and the eyebrows (oh yeah: you need to draw eyebrows), and they should be flat by the head. Then the hair – smooth it across the forehead using the top of the egg as the top of the hair. The hair does NOT start on top of the egg, because that would give you huge puffy hair like an eighties rock band.

BY EDDIE RED

3.

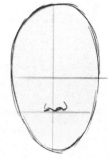

Divide the lower half of the egg again with another horizontal line. This line is where the nose "rests." Go ahead and draw the base of the nose, resting just on the top of this line.

4.

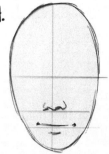

Divide the bottom quarter in half again with another horizontal line (I told you you'd be erasing later on!). The lips will rest on top of this line. Draw them in.

7.

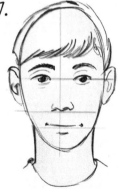

Last is the neck, which starts to appear by the jawline. Make it a sturdy neck or your head will roll off in the wind. (Not really, but a cool zombie visual, right?)

And that's it! Easy! Ha – I know, I know . . . it's tricky stuff. But keep practicing and you'll get the hang of it. This guy looks like a Karl to me. Karl the Krusher.

COMING IN SPRING 2015

Edmund and Jonah are off on a two-week family trip to Mexico, filled with parasailing, snorkeling, and sunny beaches. But when Edmund's father is accused of stealing a priceless artifact from the hotel, it's up to Eddie Red to solve the crime and save the day.

Armed with a bottle of iodine and the book *Aztec Gods and You*, the boys uncover a real-life ghost mystery, one involving an invisible alphabet, a teenage street gang, and a thief obsessed with avenging his father's death.

Whether they're fighting germs from Montezuma's revenge or battling a bad guy on top of a Mayan pyramid, they have only one important rule to follow this vacation:

Never underestimate the power of projectile vomit.

ACKNOWLEDGMENTS

So many amazing people helped make Eddie Red possible. First, a huge thanks to my ninja agent Kristin Nelson, for taking a chance on me and helping me become a better writer. Thanks also to Anita Mumm for pulling Eddie from the slush pile, and to the rest of the hard-working Nelson Literary Agency. To Ann Rider, my über-awesome editor whose kind and thoughtful approach has soothed my nerves in this wonderfully crazy process. Thank you! Thanks to Scott Magoon, Alison Kerr Miller, Mary Huot, Rachel Wasdyke, and the talented people of Houghton

Mifflin Harcourt. And thank you, Marcos Calo, for helping Eddie come to life in your wonderful illustrations.

Thanks to the hysterically funny kids and faculty of the Gailer School, who inspired me and made me laugh every day. An extra-big thanks to Mary Lower for the drawing lessons, Diane Guertin for the chess lessons, and Galen Fastie for being a patient reader.

A huge thanks to my readers: Drew Whitney, Beth Charles, Kimberly Jones, and my sisters Laura Wells and Autumn Williams—you're the best!

Thank you to my friends and family for their love and support. A special shout-out to the Wells and the Elkins families for their vast and enthusiastic knowledge of New York City, to my mom, Jeanne Williams, for her endless generosity, and to my husband, Ben, and my two kids for putting up with me and microwave dinners. Thank you for keeping me grounded and silly.

And to you, my reader. Thank you.